NIKESH SHUKLA

D0001553

QUARTET

First published in 2010 by Quartet Books Limited
A member of the Namara Group
27 Goodge Street, London W1T 2LD

A catalogue record for this book is available from the British Library

ISBN   978 0 7043 7204 7

Typeset by Antony Gray
Printed and bound in Great Britain by
T J International Ltd, Padstow, Cornwall

For my wife Katie and my *bapuji* [grandfather]
Jayantilal Jadevji Shukla.

હું આ પુસ્તક મારા દાદા
શ્રી જયંતીલાલ શુક્લા ના ચરણે મા
સમર્પીત કરુ છું.

નિકેશ શુક્લા

ACKNOWLEDGEMENTS

Katie – without your humour, support, and wishing, this book wouldn't have got written and I would have given up a long time ago. You've still got butt plums, though. HOOBA HOOBA. Bumbear Bahul, you recorded my first ever rap tape. I got ready for the megablast. You're officially *pretty cool*. Mum, Dad and sister, this book is fictional and no characters bear any resemblance to persons alive or dead . . . or do they? The entire Shukla, Rao and Pandya families have been invaluable sources of warmth, giving and stories so I apologise for any close-to-the-bone comparisons. Thanks to Niven Govinden for his feisty advice and introducing me to Gavin James Bower, who did a sterling job editing this bad boy because he's hot and fresh out the kitchen #truestory. Rob, Jeff, Tom and Nick are my hip-hop consultants, the funniest fam a man can have. Rob invented the sixth element of hip-hop: blammin'. Jeff invented the seventh element of hip-hop: iMacin'. Extra special thanks, though, to Tom for ghostwriting Verbal Sharkey's lyrics dem and Nick for covering my book.

Charlie Dark and the Run Dem Crew have given me the perfect thinking space while running the streets of London (tortoise-crew represent). Stuart Evers, you're a gentleman and your unwavering support of the book has been beautiful, like you. Nimer – oh Rashed, dear Rashed, remember Sammy Jankus. Riz MC, you're a constant inspiration, full of light, talent, warmth and energy. Rukhsana and Ailah – thanks for supporting and spreading the word at every turn. Rosemarie Hudson for invaluable mentoring. Anna Goodall, Tim Wells and the *Pen Pusher* team got me started so thanks for the sweet hook-ups.

Million billion special thanks to Salena and Rachel from Book Club Boutique, who've welcomed me into their warm bosoms and filled my womb with Sha-boom. Make light. Charles and Gemma from the Arts Council – thanks for waiting patiently. I got there eventually. Nerm, Kunal-age, Vinny the dakoo (where's your album lovetubs?), Bobby Friction, Niki Bedi, Magical Anjali, Rahul Verma, Matthew Xia, Evie Wyld, Sanjai of the Dead – you've all inspired and encouraged me in your own ways and I'm indebted to you all. This is the soppiest thing I'll say to any of you, ever.

Thank you dear reader, for reading the book (I hope you liked it) and for wading through a page of in-jokes and wittering.

Thanks to Chuck D and Flava Flav. Y*eeeeeaaaaahhhhh boyeeeee.*

London, 2010

THANKS

All lyrics by Verbal Sharkey/Herman were provided
by Vee Kay (Sweatbox Sounds).

Additional lyrics in chapter seven originally appeared in
'Step Out My Cornershop' by Yam Boy and Goonda-
Raj (*Maad Ethics* LP, 2005), written by Nurul Kabir and
Nikesh Shukla.

'Pretty Cool' featured on a Maxwell C-90 tape, recorded
by Bumbear Bahul and Nikesh Shukla, 1991.

An extract from *Coconut Unlimited* was published in
Pen Pusher issue 14.

CONTENTS

When I'm writing, I'm trapped in between the lines,
I escape when I finish the rhyme . . .
I got soul

Eric B and Rakim, 'I Got Soul'

They Reminisce Over You

The day starts quiet. The day starts slow.

I can see today's outfit, lovingly laid out for me by Alice on the small white children's chair next to the bed. I'm awake ten minutes before the alarm goes off. I stare at the clock counting towards 9 a.m. Alice's warmth has left the sheets and the flat is too quiet for her usual Saturday morning thumping around. She's left for her mother's, while I'm left in bed.

Alice has placed a note on her pillow wishing me well for today. She's left it with a Polaroid of herself, in some underwear, scribing underneath: 'JUST SO WE BOTH KNOW YOU'RE THINKING OF ME.' I smile and place it under her pillow. The day's tingling, amping me to get up, get out, do something. I bounce out of bed. Day, you are mine.

Toast. Tea. Both alleviate me. *Saturday Live* is on Radio 4. Luke Wright's reading a poem about supermarkets. There's a profile of an Argentinian goat herder who beat the death squads in the 80s.

My phone beeps the arrival of a text, distracting me. It's from Anand, saying he's going to be late. The flight's delayed so he'll be a few hours. I don't know where we're headed so I'll have to sit it out.

I consider starting on a beer but all I want's another cup of tea. I'm starting to see with all of my eye sockets now. I got accidentally drunk last night and ended up chatting about books with a guy at a gig till midnight, then I stumbled home, woke Alice up and ate leftovers in the armchair, Jools Holland in the background and my email in the foreground. Not the best day to be hungover.

I open the fridge to grab some juice and spot a cold Lucozade with a pink lip-shaped post-it note. From Alice, obviously. Thanks babe. I grab it and take a swig, allowing the fizz to lacerate my throat.

Refreshed, I head to the shower, tripping over some records I haven't put back from a few nights ago, some Velvet Underground and some old Bollywood – strange combination. The shower's lukewarm but it's throbbing with heat outside. I let it cleanse me.

Then I head back to the bedroom and start to put on my civvies. No point changing yet. I look at a photo clamped between the wall and the mirror in the bedroom. It's of Anand, Nishant and me, standing outside a restaurant called Saqee, all mugging for the camera, looking stupid. It's filled with so much life, energy and complete abandon that I want to cry.

Text messages come in from everyone else effervescing with excitement about today. It's gonna be booming, I'm promised. The plan is: grab some lunch with the boys, catch up, then head to a mystery location.

I look out of my window. I can see a film star's house from my front room, in my leafy pothole behind the grime of Finsbury Park's estates. I can see the community centre that has twelve-hour-long church sessions every Sunday. I can also see my neighbour strain to unlock his bike in the front garden, having only ever offered Alice a tight space to leave hers, meaning his bike is perfectly lodged behind. I watch him struggle a bit, and smile. I have to be careful. I'm on the ground floor and he could easily knock on my window, as he's done before, and get me to move her bike. I don't have her keys today, fuckwad, so I'll watch you struggle.

To get myself in the mood, I put on a Ghostface Killah album and sway and nod my head and smile, pointing my gun hands at imaginary crowds, seeing them before me. The curtains are open, but I don't care if anyone sees me enthusiastically yelping out half-remembered rap lyrics. This is my day.

Bang! I'm launching into 'RUN!' by Ghostface and Jadakiss when the buzzer sounds, a deep sonic woof into the belly of the flat, erupting and shocking everything in its wake. I put my tea down, before turning the hi-fi off. It's probably the postman with a package. I grab my keys, in case the door swings closed as it's prone to do, and run out into the corridor. I can see some sort of red monstrosity in the opaque window of the door. It doesn't look like the postman. Red button clicked, door swung open . . .

'BRRRRRRRRRRAAAAAAAAAAPPPPPPPPPPPPPPP!' Anand bellows, resplendent in red. He's throwing up the 'Blood' gang sign with his contorted fingers, wearing a bandana, fake gold grills in his teeth, his red T-shirt peppered with bullet holes. 'Yeeeeeeeeaaaaaaaaaahhhhhhhhhhh!' He smiles.

'I'm not even ready yet bro!'

'Word up homes,' he says in a fake American accent. I look beyond him.

'Where's . . . I thought you were at the . . . '

Out of the blind spot of the front garden moonwalks Nishant, booming tall, barrel-chested and beaming, his grey eyes set into chubby, pinchable cheeks, his hair still bed-headed. He's wearing a red shirt, leather jacket, a bandana round his neck like a cowboy, leather shoes and jeans. He glides past Anand, does a 180 degree turn and spins into my outstretched arms.

'YOOOOO!' he yells, hugging me.

'HOLLAAAAAAAAAAAAA!'

I pound them both with hugs and bring them in together, silent and joyful.

'Nice digs,' Nishant says.

'When did you get in man?' I ask.

'Yesterday.'

'WHAT?'

'Yeah man, I came a day earlier. Didn't want to be tired for your big day.'

'Thanks . . . '

'Anand let me stay in his filthy flat. He needs a girlfriend.'

'What girlfriend would let him live like that?' I say, smiling.

'Yeah yeah, guys, fuck you very much. Let's get Mit Dogg changed and out for lunch and on the beers . . . and then to his last night of freedom!' Anand's a bundle of electricity.

'Were you listening to Ghostface when we came down the driveaway?'

'Good ears Nishant.'

'You still love it after all these years . . . '

'Man, what can I say? It's in me.'

'Amit go get changed!' Anand screams. 'We'll do the gay catching up thing at the pub.'

I beckon them into the living room. Anand, a veteran of my flat, kicks his shoes off and sets about making a cup of tea for himself, and a hot water with lemon and honey for Nishant.

I retreat to the bedroom, kick off my clothes and prepare for the abomination Alice made last night. The theme for the stag-do is Bloods vs Crips and we're Bloods. She's sewed 'BRRRAP' onto my red basketball vest in some gold thread she had left over from Christmas. I'm not proud of it but it's endearingly her, so I put it on, then find my baggy jeans from school, amazed I can still fit into them, if I push back with my bum, lean forward and suck the tightest of tight breaths. My shoes are my old Nikes. My socks are my red football socks. I roll one leg up and put on the bandana, rolled crisply round my head so the knot's at the front. The years of careful study have amounted to something. Finally, I have a use for my teenage obsession with LA gangs.

I walk in on Anand telling Nishant an animated story about pulling a girl, and I stare at them, smiling, gripping the remnants of my lukewarm tea in the cup of my hands. Anand's a static picture of our teenage years, while Nishant looks at peace with himself, with his body, with his mind, with Anand – with life in general. Anand still has that buzz of chaos about him, the hum of nervous energy that always threatened to spill into hissy fits or noise-pollutions.

Nishant catches me watching and smiles.

'It's you.'

Anand mutters something about Alice's middle class interpret-ation of gangsta, and Nishant pinches his side as he rises off the sofa. He leads us both out, placing his drink on the dining table. He turns back at the door.

'It's going to be a great day.'

'Yes indeed . . . '

'Let's go you gays.' Anand ushers us out into the crispy summer day, the pound of heat on the concrete carpet, the yummy mummies and banking daddies of Crouch End bustling past.

I place an arm around Nishant and lean into his armpit as he receives me. We do the sideways squeeze.

Then we climb into Anand's car. He's planning to drive us to lunch before ditching the car and going feral with beers. At least that's what he's told us. What he hasn't told us is that it's really nice to see us both, which is why he keeps calling us 'gay'.

I look at them both and try to remember the last time we were all together. It's been years. Tinges of memory flutter through me. I'm sleek with the promise of the day and overwhelmed with the presence of my two best friends. Memories all melt into one.

I sit down in the car, close the door and then my eyes. Anand bundles in, shaking everything in his wake, pressing 'play' on the car stereo.

DON'T-DON'T-DON'T DON'T BELIEVE THE HYPE . . . HOOOYYYUUURRR . . .

It's Public Enemy. I open my eyes and nod at him in appreciation.

'You remember this?' he yells over the music.

'Of course man . . . '

How could I forget? That song, it started everything.

Next: Step In the Arena

CHAPTER ONE

Don't Believe The Hype

One summer when I was nine and Neel was eleven, we had a tape. It was one of those Maxwell C-90 tapes, brown with silver stickering, spools squeaky from overuse. He'd written on it in scrawly blue biro: 'Rap Trax!' I couldn't work out if the exclamation mark was his or the album's. The 'X' seemed so abbreviating, so exciting, so dangerous. It was a simple anarchic act that went against all of my private school upbringing. The streets were coming to Harrow.

Neel was my cousin. He lived in Croydon, away from the rest of our family. Every summer, his mum would send him to stay with his grandma, our ba, in Harrow to learn Gujarati. I hero-worshipped him. He was a complete nerd but self-assured and confident – an expert at chess with a labyrinthian knowledge of UK comedy. We'd lie on our fronts and read our comics together, while my ba watched her Bollywood tapes, the only time she'd see us all summer outside of meals.

Ba had a tape player in her bedroom, which we used to record our voices. We'd sit up there for hours with blank tapes, press 'record' and say whatever came into our minds, occasionally choosing to script things, giving them a proper narrative. They veered from rehashes of our favourite bits from sitcoms like *'Allo 'Allo!* or *Only Fools and Horses* to postmodern skits involving characters pooled from all our favourite TV shows.

That day, though, Neel held up 'Rap Trax!' He put it in the tape recorder and pressed 'play'. We had those first five seconds of tape silence before it spooled into the uneven crunch of a warm vinyl crackle. Our other cousin Nishu, who lived in Southall with all the real Asians, had decks and records and was about five years older than Neel. He'd recorded this album for him.

And it was then that . . . my ears bled . . . my head exploded . . . my heart started beating.

A fuzzy distorted horse-neigh twisted into a repetitive sample, a booming kick drum thudding against my diaphragm, snares snapping like slaps to my face.

DON'T-DON'T-DON'T BELIEVE THE HYPE (wooooo-ahhhhhwwwahhhhh) . . .

'Who's this?' I asked.

'Public Enemy,' Neel said, nodding.

> *Back*
> *Caught you lookin' for the same thing*
> *It's a new thing check out this I bring*
> *Uh Oh the roll below the level*
> *'Cause I'm livin' low next to the bass*
> *C'mon*
> *Turn up the radio*

What were they talking about?

'Neel . . . what are they talking about?'

'Not believing the hype.' Neel was a master at presenting vagueness as confident commentary.

'I don't get it.'

'It's just politics stuff. You know . . . '

I wanted to remain cool. Instead my heart was trying to burst out of my chest. My mind was trying to pump its righteous fist in indignation. My feet wanted to tap. I didn't want to display too much uncool emotion but noticed Neel was tapping his foot between the kick drum and the snare, so I followed. We stumbled into an awkward rhythm – first, KRS-One, then Eric B and Rakim, then Whodini, then Kid'n'Play. My mind was fizzing, filled with the spirit of black power and black rage and black funk and black edu-tainment. It rendered me speechless. Neel was lost in a trance, his feet tapping and his head nodding independently of each other, and the beat. I stole looks at what he was doing and tried to focus on the words, what they were saying in the strange spoken lyrics, the 'rap'.

'We should write our own,' said Neel.

'OK, but I need to record this off you.'

'No problem. Got a tape?'

I always had blank tapes with me, just in case I needed to blam something off the radio or an impromptu radio play presented itself. I pulled it out. It was one of Dad's old Bollywood tapes that I hadn't heard him listen to in ages. I handed it over. The tabs were broken, meaning it couldn't be recorded over. Neel pulled a tissue out from next to Ba's bed and tore off two bits, rolling them into balls, filling the tape gaps. He put the tape in the second deck, rewound 'Rap Trax!' to the beginning and put the volume down so it wouldn't interrupt the new scheme he was planning. He pressed 'record'. 'Rap Trax!' was ninety minutes away from being mine.

'We should write our own,' he said again, more urgently this time.

'Definite.'

'I've been studying beatbox.'

'What's beatbox?'

'You don't know?'

'Erm, no . . . '

'You've got a lot to learn . . . ' he said, shaking his head. 'Beatbox is where you make the noises of the drum in your mouth. Like this . . . *pu-tu-pitpit-papu-tu-pitpit* . . . get it?' He continued his demonstration.

Pu-tu-pitpit-papu-tu-pitpit . . .
Pu-tu-pitpit-papu-tu-pitpit . . .
Pu-tu-pitpit-papu-tu-pitpit . . .

He stopped. 'Aren't you going to rap over the beatbox?'

'I don't know how.'

'So much to learn . . . '

While 'Rap Trax!' recorded, Neel found some scrap paper and we started writing our first lyrics. Bandying about subject matter and title, we got stuck on the idea of 'cool', so my first rap song became 'Pretty Cool'. It was a symbol of our confidence. We weren't awesome cool or mega cool. We were only . . . *pretty cool.*

Neel wrote the whole thing. I hadn't grasped rhythm and rhyming enough to feel confident, plus I bowed to his superior knowledge about rap so I just sat there as his nodding agree-machine.

> *My name's Amit I got to school*
> *I got loadsa friends and I'm pretty cool*

My name's Neel, I never steal
And I've got the real deal

> *There was a girl I used to like*
> *She was fine she was just my type*

Then I found out she told a lie
She was going out with another guy

We had to do it in one take, with Neel beatboxing during my bit, then me tap-tap-tapping on a chair near the speaker during his, and then, during the chorus, both of us tap-tap-tapping on the chair for double emphasis.

> *We're pretty cool, don't be a fool,*
> *Don't go to school, don't be a fool . . .*

We played it back. The tap-tap-tap sounded like someone flicking the speaker with their nail and was dominating the sound, pushing Neel's vocals to the back of the mix. He screwed up his nose.

'Sounds good, man,' I offered.

'No it doesn't. It sounds whack. We need to have me beatboxing all the way through. Otherwise the bits without it sound whack, homeboy.'

'Erm . . . '

'How are we going to make it less whack?'

'Well . . . ' I thought hard. I needed to be the one with the solution so I looked *pretty cool.* 'Ba has another tape recorder downstairs. What if we record you beatboxing onto one tape and then we play it on the other tape recorder and rap along and the recorder'll pick up both of us *and* the beatboxing . . . '

'That's dope! Except . . . '

'Except what . . . ?'

'We need another tape . . wait, we'll borrow one from Ba!'

I was sent downstairs to negotiate. My pidgin Gujarati was better than Neel's as I could communicate through my lack of vocabulary without getting flustered. The rule with Gujarati was, as a regional dialect, it had never been updated to include more modern words like 'toilet' or 'hip-hop' or 'fork', so you could form the sentences around English nouns with ease and Ba would understand you. As long as the verbs and gender-specific addresses were fine, she had no cause for complaint. She said words like 'television' and 'food processor' and 'cheese' to mean things like . . . television and food processor and cheese, but without compromising her humble Gujarati upbringing.

'Ba . . . ?' I said.

'Ha, beta?' [Yes, darling?]

'Mune tumaro tape recorder borrow kuru che?' [Can I borrow your tape recorder?]

Amazingly, the Gujarati word for 'please' doesn't really exist as there's never cause to use it, so I just said in a humble Gujarati accent: '*Please* . . . ?'

'Sena mate, beta?' [What for, darling?]

'Ooopur, recording kuru che.' [We want to do some recording upstairs.]

'Su?' [What?]

'Hip-hop nu song.' [A hip-hop song.]

'Aa hip-hop su che?' [What's hip-hop?]

'Ba, mane tape recorder borrow kuru che!' [Ba, I want to borrow the tape recorder!]

'OK.'

I ran upstairs with the tape recorder. Neel was waiting for me at the edge of the bed, gargling some spit in the front of his mouth to keep his teeth moist so he could rock the beatbox. I placed the tape recorder on the bed and plugged it in. Neel pressed eject.

'There's a tape already in here,' he said.

'We should ask first . . . '

'No, we'll just use two minutes of it at the end. She'll never notice. Just blame it on me. I'm used to it.'

The end of side two had about ten minutes blank. Neel moistened his lips. I hit 'record'.

He beatboxed his heart out, wavering in and out of time, struggling to keep enough moisture in his mouth to get through it. I managed to hit 'stop' at the end of the beatbox before he erupted into coughs. It was the same pattern throughout the song but we recorded it with enough time and space so the beatbox would start with my first line and end with the last line of the second run-through of our chorus. Because we were professionals. Neel coached me through the simple rhythm so we could record the vocals in one take. It *was* going to be *pretty cool.*

We got through the recording and listened back in anticipation. Up until this point, my life had never been that exciting. Now, life had reached a new pinnacle. It was a real 'Dear Diary' moment. I felt so *pretty cool.* My first ever rap record – a rabid runthrough of why I was awesome. Like the braggadocious masters Kool Keith and Rakim, I knew I had soul.

The next evening, Ba had some of the local Gujarati community round her house for weekly prayers. They would sing tunelessly to the Gods and take stake in the customs they'd imported to England. The night usually finished with a tape recording of the *Hanuman Chalisa*, as recorded by supreme Bollywood superstar Amitabh Bachchan.

As the final verse faded out there was the chewed crackle of a new recording, and Neel's voice boom-bapping into a room of middle class Gujaratis sitting in cross-legged contemplation.

25

Pu-tis-pa-tis

Pu-tis-pa-tis

Pu-tis-pa-tis

Pu-tis-pa-tis

Pu-tis-pa-tis

Pu-tis-pa-tis

Pu-tis-pa-tis

Pu-tis-pa-tis

Neel and I listened from the stairs, giggling to ourselves.

*   *   *

Being the only three brown kids in a practically all-white private school, my best friends Anand, Nishant and I were considered stereotypical Asians. Meanwhile, our Asian peers on the other side of town thought we wanted to be white. The only way to keep it rugged and real, to do something for ourselves, was to set up a hip-hop band. My childhood obsession with rap influencing Anand and Nishant's tastes, away from pop and Michael Jackson, was just what our friendship needed. There was no other option.

I was the natural born leader, the smooth-talker, the most/least confident one, the one with the most to prove. Then there was Anand, small, loud and fierce, agreeable and agreeing, trend-spotting and trend-plotting, and fiercely loyal. And then there was Nishant, laconic and lackadaisical, mature and immature, wide-eyed and wise, and obsessive, the sweet backbone. We were a triple threat: smooth, energetic and sweet.

I was the frontman, naturally. Anand was going to be the hype-man and Nishant, who couldn't rap, volunteered to be the DJ, because it was the only role going and his dad had a turntable. It never occurred to me to have it any other way. Anand assumed that the hypeman had half the work and the same glory as the frontman, and Nishant was just happy to be involved in some way. Anand couldn't wait to get started and he was a bundle of feverish learning, absorbing everything he could find about hip-hop and top hype-men. Nishant, obsessed with Michael Jackson, thought that being the DJ would give him ample space to dance his heart out. I just wanted to make the girls scream and show up our school friends.

Nishant's dad didn't play his records till around ten at night, so there was all that time after school to monopolise the stereo. In the days before we owned any wax vinyl, I'd stick on taped classics we liked by KRS-One and Rakim and Chuck D, and try to rap along, mimicking the US accents, skipping over the times they uttered the 'N' bomb, trying to catch the rhythm . . . any rhythm at all. Anand would practise his fierce face in the mirror and Nishant would try to perfect his breakdancing.

We had no musical training between us. I had no clue about drum-beats or rapping over them. Nishant had no idea of how to beat-match two records, seeing as his dad only owned one turntable, let alone scratch. Only Anand felt comfortable in his role, which would amount to not much more than shouting 'YEAA AAAH BOY!' every now and then.

We spent months listening to the same few tapes, sent through the post from Neel. I didn't know where to go and buy hip-hop records - Harrow only stocked indie - but the more I thought about being in a band, the more the idea became cemented in my head as something we just had to do. Like I said, there was no other option.

In the dying days of summer, feeling anxious about a new school year ahead, about returning to the same fractious relationships we'd happily avoided for two months, the same banter-masking-mickey-taking and general annoyance at our presence, the band started to mean everything, although it seemed that the last thing on our minds was actually making any music.

'Yo, bredren, we be the illest,' went my proclamation.

'We be the dopest,' Anand would follow.

'Our tunes are going to be good,' Nishant would finish with.

The band had mystique before melody. It was a series of ideas for look and feel, logos and album titles. It was an abstract wind of change.

We had no songs.

The name came from my sister. She'd laugh at us and would ask questions like, 'Do you even know who Aamir Khan is?' before dissolving into embarrassed mirth. We'd shrug and she'd giggle like a baby, finding it so funny that we were unaware of the existence of this Bollywood hunk.

'Shut up,' I'd counter. 'You're so Asian. You only like Indian food and watch Bollywood. You're so sad. I bet you don't even know who Scott La Rock is.'

'You're so white,' she'd laugh back. 'You're white on the inside, brown on the outside . . . like coconuts!'

When I told Anand this, he decided it needed to be our statement of intent. Then, after hours of naming loads of other qualifiers – 'Crew', 'Gang', 'Clique', 'Posse' – we plucked the name 'Unlimited' out of the air, and it stuck. We'd jot down our ideas on scrap-paper from Dad's old warehouse supplies, scrap-paper that still bore the 80s logo for his company, ending with 'Limited'. We were Unlimited, though. We were *Coconut Unlimited.*

The name took on a shamanic quality. I wrote it everywhere, doodled it on every notebook, library book, bus stop – any surface that would allow a hasty Biro, felt-tip or colouring pencil. Margins of paper that I tried to write lyrics on contained elaborate designs for logos, either written as tags or in calligraphy or superheroic Marvel lettering, or just plain old-fashioned capitals. Nishant, the only one of us who could draw, would sketch hip-hop-type b-boys and breakdancers with 'Coconut Unlimited' written on their chests in Wyld Style lettering. I was so excited about the name. Coconuts and proud.

During one of our many 'Cocon-ferences' Nishant said, 'Do we really want to be Coconut Unlimited with Amit, Anand and Nishant?'

'I get what you're saying,' said Anand.

'We should have rugged names,' he continued. 'I need a dangerous DJ name.'

'Definitely. So, what kinda name do you want?'

'Something definite.'

'DJ Definite?' Anand suggested.

'No. Something more street and edgy.'

'Yeah, definite. DJ Edge? What about me?'

Nishant took one look at Anand, screwing up his pop-eye.

'MC Dangerous?'

'Guys . . . I have the perfect name for me,' I declared, interrupting their brainstorm. 'Mit Dogg.'

They paused and considered it.

'Definite.'

You just couldn't argue with Mit Dogg. That was a heavy hitter name. I sat back, pleased with myself.

'If you're Mit Dogg, I wanna be MC AP,' said Anand, using his initials. Anand had recently noticed the proliferation of initials in hip-hop names and he was nothing if not a trend-spotter.

'Well if no one's using Dangerous, I'll be DJ Dangerous.' Nishant smiled, glad to reclaim the only decent name in the running as far as he was concerned.

'Right,' declared Anand. 'MC AP, DJ Dangerous, Mit Dogg . . . It's probably about time we wrote some raps for Coconut Unlimited.'

'Definite.'

* * *

MC AP, DJ Dangerous and I were walking the 300-metre stretch between AP's house and the shops, brainstorming our band identity.

'We should all wear the same stuff,' said Anand. 'The exact same outfits, like rappers do.'

'Yeah good idea AP,' I said. 'Like denim jeans and denim jackets . . .'

'What about just white vests and denim jeans?'

'A bit more rugged. Good idea Dangerous.'

We were on our way to a newsagent's who stocked *Hip-Hop Connection*, and another magazine called *The Source*. Both hip-hop magazines were our suburban guide to the gritty pyrotechnics of inner-city American youth music.

Hip-Hop Connection reviewed albums and interviewed rap stars in a classically British way, reverential but sarcastic, never really talking about the music, always tonguing its cheek in tone and look. *The Source*, an American mag, talked about revolution and painted rap stars in mythical pedestal shades, while maintaining a high advertising space to editorial ratio throughout with heavily stylised photoshoots and earnest reportage on the textures of the music. Most importantly, though, the American mag printed lyrics, which we could study and learn.

'We have to study the greats if we're going to get good,' said Anand.

'Exactly AP,' I said, nodding sagely.

'What, like Michael Jackson?' asked Nishant.

'No,' I scoffed. 'Like Onyx and Ice-T and stuff.'

'Oh right . . . but that Michael Jackson song, the one with that *Home Alone* kid, has some rapping doesn't it?'

'Not proper rapping from, like, The Bronx or LA or anything.' I needed to nip this in the bud, and toughen him up. He was my Terminator X, not my Quincy Jones.

'Where's the Neverland ranch anyway? I'm sure it's near LA . . . '

'Oh whatever Nishant,' I said, shaking my head.

'Erm, I thought you were supposed to call me Dangerous . . . ?'

We arrived at the newsagent's. Before going in, I took a pound each off them to procure the magazine, this week *The Source*, and entered, the bell dinging our arrival. Anand pounced on the penny sweets while I grabbed *The Source*, pointing up at me like a beacon of righteousness, Gang Starr standing proudly on the cover like . . . well, gangsters. Nishant hovered by the front of the shop near the magazine rack. I stood behind Anand as he counted out his daily quota of cola cubes, his teeth yellowed, salivating with the next fix being prepared in front of him. Sugar gleamed off the counter, powdered residue from the tubs like a Scarface amount of yayo. This fetishistic process took a while, so I flicked through the magazine to see what the lyrics were this month: 'Nuttin' But a 'G' Thang' by Dr Dre and Snoop Doggy Dogg. Awesome. I tried to read it out, stumbling over some of the slang.

What did 'loc'd out' mean? Where was Long Beach? Was that in California? 'Pull a strap out the cut' – what was all that about?

It was the illusion of danger that excited me. That summer, as we prepared to enter our GCSE years, we were starting to feel like our imprisonment in the suburbs was ending. At private school, the only thing to rebel against was wealth, which made all the white kids turn to angsty guitar music about upset stomachs and feelings of parental resentment. We three had no wealth to rebel against. We were the victims of our parents' desire to ensure we had a good education, meaning all their money was spent on private school. No holidays, no proper nights out, no musical instruments, no frivolity – only austere learning. We rebelled against the stigma of being the three Asians.

In our fictional social system we were the penniless, despite our privileged education, and thus aligned ourselves with the streets, in particular the streets of Compton and the Bronx. So, to prove to ourselves we weren't coconuts, we tried to be brown on the outside and black in the middle. We knew we had soul, and hip-hop was our way of showing it. The worst thing for us, it seemed, was to be called wealthy and posh by our Asian peers, and equals by our white peers. We needed to be dirty and rugged, to maintain the oppression of our race, and hip-hop was perfect for that.

Anand finished up his cola cube transaction. I stepped up and slammed three pound coins on the counter like an oppressed inner-city youth born with the skills of rhythm and rhyme. The shop owner tutted and handed me my change. I nodded upwards twice, lightening quick, and walked back to where Nishant and now Anand were standing. They were grinning, Nishant holding something behind his back and shaking his six-foot frame with a mirth that was barely containable. The shopkeeper had returned to the cricket on a television that he kept under the counter.

'What's up?'

Nishant swirled round. He was holding *Knave* magazine, looking at a girl stretching her smooth opening as far as she could, her mouth frozen for infinity in the 'o' of simulated satisfaction.

'Check that out.'

'It's called a shaven haven,' said Anand, as if this was supposed to be the thing that caught my perverse teenage attention.

'You guys need to grow up,' I said, shaking my head.

'What? Look at her, you can see all the way up to the top.'

'To her brain!'

'Yeah but if we get good,' I said, 'we could see for real . . . '

'I get you,' nodded MC AP, snatching the magazine from Nishant's clammy fingers and placing it next to *Angler's Weekly* – the bravado back in place, unruffled.

'Her specifically?' asked Nishant.

'Better.'

'Better?'

'Better.'

We left, heading for the benches in the car park by the super-market, where we could read the magazine in turn. None of us had heard of the bands in this month's issue. Large Professor? Craig Mack? Who *were* these guys?

'Tell me about Gang Starr,' said Nishant, in an effort to start a conversation I'd be interested in.

'One MC, one DJ . . . '

'Classic combo,' Anand affirmed.

'No hype man?'

'No.'

'What do we need Anand for?' Nishant shrugged, ever the pragmatist, never the catcher of feelings.

I continued to precis the interview with Gang Starr for the boys, skipping over the boring stuff like what sound they were going for, focusing instead on Guru's life on the streets and DJ Premier's scratching methods, giving them the broad strokes. Once scanned, I turned to the other most important thing in *The Source* (number one being lyrics): the album of the month. I read it with interest, trying to hear the music in my head as they described it. Nishant interrupted my meditation.

'What should our first song be about?'

'It should be a mission statement or something.'

'About how we're coconuts?'

'Nah, no one cares about why we'd prefer to be white over brown.'

I sat in silence, thinking, while Anand and Nishant went over the finer points of relevant subject matter.

'Something about getting girls?'

'No, something about ripping someone's head off and spitting in the wound.'

'What about getting a girl, then her boyfriend tries to give you trouble . . . *then* you do the head ripping spitting death move?' Nishant offered.

'That's awesome man.'

'Yeah awesome, like . . . *I rip your head off, man, spit in the wound cos that's the plan.*'

I was silent, my brain farting out half ideas and words, but I had nothing. Anand stopped and looked at me for assurance. I nodded and smiled.

'*I rip your head off, man, spit in the wound cos that's the plan.* That could be the chorus.'

'Yeah man. That's dangerous.'

'I got it.' They both turned to me. 'We write about how we got the whole world fooled. We're really the gangsters round here.

We're the ones people should be afraid of, cos we got the moves and the guns and the drugs and stuff.'

'Yeah, but we don't have guns and drugs and stuff . . . '

'And we can't do any death moves like we're on *Mortal Kombat* either. What's the difference?'

'*I got the moves, the guns and drugs man, got the whole world fooled cos that's the plan.*' Anand sat up proudly with his new set of lyrics.

'We might need to work on it a bit.'

*　　*　　*

I was now consumed by hip-hop, I needed to know everything about it. When I was 13 and starting to like cool personalities like Ice Cube and Ice T, I kept a notebook of every rapper and rap band I came across. Sometimes I'd make up names I thought would be good for a rapper, just to have a new entry, like:

Mista Bee

7even Heaven Devin

Cool Ass Gang

Kung Fu Fightaz

Original Pranksta

Natural Born Rappers

Rap Twins

This way I could track bands I needed to know about. Anything vaguely rap-related, I checked out, scouring newspapers and TV channels for signs of that rebellious music, anything with swearing, like Onyx with their *Bacdafucup* album. Often the names I wrote down had no grounding in reality. I didn't know their music, I didn't know their style, I didn't know what they looked like – they just existed as a bunch of names, a petition-sized list of rappers.

I loved anything political. I was at that awkward stage of starting to feel like I understood how the world worked without knowing how the world worked. I had that fire in my belly. That vague notion of politics. I loved soundbite statements of intent. I was the annoying teenager who'd declare all war wrong and completely unjustifiable at all times. No grey, only shades of brown and white.

I was proud to be brown in my own way. Well, I was at school; at school I was brown about the funky stuff that came with being vegetarian, like being really arrogant about it, declaring proudly to a room full of beefeaters when Mad Cow disease initially broke that it was 'Vishnu's way of telling y'all to stop eating and start worshipping'. When I was thirteen and obsessed with drawing, my pre-making-music obsession, I'd drawn a comic set in post-apocalyptic India called *Hindustan* where the Shahs and Khans fought futuristic dystopian battles over scorched landscapes. This was at a time when the Muslim/Hindu troubles had hit fever pitch and, not knowing any of the history, I sided privately with the Hindus, never telling my Muslim childhood friend Junaid. He'd never see the comic and we'd never talk about it, but the precedent had been set: I was privately very proud of my Indianness, while publicly I was aloof and as Bronx-like as possible with my Asian peers.

It was with these vague abstractions of self and identity that I bought into the political polemic of heavy rap, its sound like distortion raining revolution over our bellies, stoking fires and loc'ing liars.

Anand loved the summery stuff. He'd made the transition from pop to rap quite easily, by broaching it through poppier records by Jazzy Jeff and the Fresh Prince and Snow. But the one record that had made him sit up and get funky with it was Skee-Lo's 'I Wish I Was a Little Bit Taller'. Anand was the shortest kid in our class, and the darkest. Skee-Lo was short too, and he sang to the summery short man syndrome lying dormant in Anand's soul, with his empowering call to tiny nerds across the world to unite and get that girl.

I wish I was little bit taller
I wish I was a baller
I wish I had a girl who looked good
I would call her
I wish I had a rabbit in a hat with a bat
And a '64 Impala

Anand wasn't a fan of the rugged stuff like me. He preferred music with no hint of tension. Even the gangsta rap he favoured featured sun-drenched violence, violence bedraggled by the laconic sunstroked personas behind it. There wasn't much fear in the lazy synths and bouncing basslines made for happy music away from the tense terse shenanigans happening up and down the East Coast, that studied parrot of inner-city depravity and desolation paraded around like party music. Plus, as Anand convincingly argued, most girls liked the funky stuff, the summery, booty-bouncing hip-hop.

'No they don't,' I snorted. 'All the girls we know like miserable indie like Radiohead. All that rubbish white boys with guitars music.'

'I'm not talking about girls from Harrow. I'm talking about Indian girls from Harrow. They like all that r'n'b stuff.'

'So? Boo that . . . it's horrible.'

'No, bruv, like, these girls are into the summery hip-hop too. They, like, grind their butts and stuff. You should come down Moonlightin' next time . . . '

Moonlightin' was an r'n'b club in Harrow that had a bhangra night every Thursday. I'd never gone, partly due to my parents, partly due to the embarrassment of being in a club with only Asians listening to insipid r'n'b and cheesy bhangra, and partly because I probably wouldn't have got in. Anand went with his sister, who was older and fed him into a network of older girls, giving him a distorted view of Asian Harrow; these were older, more mature and less like my sister than I gave his stories credit for. He insisted he pulled on average every other week, bemoaning that, if he was six-foot-nine, he'd be pulling every single night. Hence the love of the summery hip-hop jams, the afterbirth of rap's evolution in my eyes. G-funk had no revolution in its belly, and no relevance to me. If it wasn't talking about Marcus Garvey or Malcolm X or police brutality, it had no bearing on my life.

Nishant was a Michael Jackson obsessive. He allowed his passing interest in hip-hop to overcome him so he could continue to hang out with Anand. He and Anand had grown up together and were thick as thieves. I was the newbie and had inserted myself with some force into their two-man gang. Initially, when they'd joined the school, relegating me from the only Asian to one of three, I was initially dubious and didn't want to know them. I made fun of them behind their backs, not only because they were Asian but because they were best friends and always stuck together, loyal to a fault. After realising that the purity of their bond was karmically better than fostering cynicism, I made nice. They accepted me but I always got the sense Nishant would rather it just be Anand and him. I'd phone them both up every night to talk plans and this became habit well into our fourteenth year. Nishant would listen in as I spouted obsessively about hip-hop, talking about themes and American inner-city geography like I was a ghetto expert. When Nishant would take the phone into his room, I'd hear a tape recorder fumble, Michael Jackson switch off and a muffled recording of my 'Rap Trax!' start up.

Nishant was the tallest and most beautiful. He was the one of whom my mum would dreamily say, 'That boy vill break lots of hearts in the growing up vhen he does' – and I'd cringe, thinking she fancied him.

Nishant could dance too. He had long gangly limbs, which he somehow managed to command, moving with determination and panache, like he was in control of his body. We were starting to slow down in our growth, instead growing outwards in beards and pubes and balls and pustules but he was the only one who felt comfortable in his skin. I always felt fat because, no matter how much exercise I did, I still had protusions on my chest and puppy fat teenage man boobs I'd never lose.

Anand, meanwhile, was short with thick hair that no matter how much he gelled and tried to hyper-style would never do what he wanted. He had a defined natural middle parting that he tried to force into an elaborate side parting with a huge Elvis quiff. Throughout the day, though, the hair would slowly creep up his scalp into the centre, where it belonged.

Nishant was a natural scruff, though, and it was the sleepiness in his big grey eyes measured against the almond skin covering his bones that made him so irresistible to mothers across Middlesex.

*   *   *

The last day before summer ended, we were all at a Gujarati social event in Wembley, in a school hall behind the high street. We were now, the three of us, the older part of the younger generation. The sixteen-to-eighteen year olds had now disappeared to the pub for beers and fags, or were old enough to convince their parents they didn't need to go to Gujarati social events in Wembley, with their embarrassing medley of saris and curries and loads of bad metallic grey suits and moustaches. So it was left to Anand, Nishant and me to be seen as the cool ones.

Except, we weren't the cool ones. We were the private school kids, and our peers went to various state schools across Wembley and Harrow and considered us all posh boys undeserving of their time.

Ravi, who was 13 and an up-and-comer on the Gujarati scene and treasurer of the Young Gujaratis of North West London Society, approached us, probably on another recruitment drive. We were the coconuts, the outcasts, the wealthy kids. Ravi was a real Asian in the eyes of the Gujarati community, a pillar of excellence held up by my parents as a comparative example of what I could be. I was going to be a musician, a famous rapper; Ravi was aiming for engineering, a life choice determined early on by a spiritual sense of responsibility and adherence to the ideal of the 'sensible job'.

Ravi, my sister told me in whisps of fancying, was a proper Indian. 'Not a bounty like you . . . you should be like him.'

'You know we're related, don't you?'

'Shut up!' she'd scream.

'Hari aum boys,' he said as he approached. 'Jay shree Krishna.' He held up prayer hands as a greeting. We'd taken up our positions on the benches between the school hall and a newly-installed outdoor basketball court. Being hip-hoppers, we were obliged to be obsessed with basketball. None of us had a ball.

'Whaa blow Ravi,' I responded. The other two raised their heads.

'Listen, do you want to take part in the talent show later?'

Anand looked up. 'The what?' he asked with a snarl.

'The youth talent show. For the YGs . . . '

'What's a YG?' asked Nishant innocently.

'Young Gujaratis,' Ravi said, tutting. 'We're the Young Gujaratis of North West London Society.'

'Nah we're cool R,' I answered dismissively.

'Well, we all thought you could do one of your raps or something if you wanted. Do something a little different.'

'What? Here?' said Anand, exasperated.

'Yeah here. You never seen the talent show before?'

'Yeah, course man,' Anand replied. 'Just surprised you're asking . . . '

'Well, the YGs feel it's important to represent all the hobbies of the community. You guys like that black music don't you?'

'What did you say?' I demanded, jumping back in.

'What? I said *rap* music . . . '

'No you didn't. You called it *black* music. Are you a racist Ravi? Are the YGs a big bunch of racists?'

'Nah man, you misheard me. I definitely said *rap.*'

'Ravi, you big massive racist. Rap is the music of revolution. Rap is the reason we have rights. If they didn't invent rap to be the

39

black man's bush telegraph, then we wouldn't know half of the shit the white man does to us.' I was incensed.

'We're not black, you idiot,' replied Ravi. 'We're Young Gujaratis.'

'We're all politically black, Ravi,' I said, righting his wrong. 'Politically, we're black and they're white. Get yourself educated.' I looked at the basketball net while telling him this, not giving him the respect of my eyes.

'Listen, just do what you want, you wannabes.' Ravi walked off.

Nishant looked up into the school hall. 'That went well,' he murmured.

'These guys just ain't ready,' I snarfed.

And with that declaration the dying embers of summer died out, our righteous revolutionary indignation burning a hole in a school bench in Wembley, a world away from the South Bronx, where our hearts resided.

Next: School Daze

CHAPTER TWO

Edutainment

The first day of term was a rush of excitement. It was usually the second or third day that filled me with dread, but the first was a brick wall waiting to be graffiti'd with spray paint. Seeing everyone again, advancing up the school food chain, amassing more social privileges as you went – these were exciting prospects.

This year, we were entering the GCSE zone. My parents, as well as Anand's, ensured we realised how important these exams were and how privileged we were to be doing them, and that we had to justify their investment. Whereas Nishant's parents chose a private school because of the access to art and culture – something they were happy to indulge their eldest child in – Anand and me, we had the fear.

Were we going to get straight As? No pressure.

Were we heading to a decent university, preferably in London – so we didn't fly the nest completely – to do a degree with transferable skills into good stable employment, with a high salary, in a recession-proof profession? No pressure.

Were we destined to validate the only Asian representation in the school through continued success? No pressure.

How to measure success, though? Anand and I were interested in social success, the success of your peers thinking you were *pretty cool*. Nishant was interested in ornithology. Our parents were interested in grades and straight As and exam statistics, as was the school. The school relied on us, being from what our headmaster referred to as a 'superiorly clever race', to get top grades. Because the school was a private school, which didn't necessarily denote intelligence, only bags of money – my Latin

41

teacher called the school 'Chequebook Academy' – entry standards weren't high. Profits over prophets.

So, it was up to us to lead the way and get the grades and show how successful the school was at dealing with multiculturalism.

No pressure.

Contrary to the stereotypes set forth by our ancestors, we all sucked at the sciences and maths. Anand was predisposed to history, Nishant to art, drama and dance and me to languages: English, French, German and Latin. I was multilingual, and probably the only Asian kid in the country who knew Latin.

That summer, though, we decided it was all about hip-hop, and the yearning for social success triumphed.

'Hi, I'm Ahmed.'

I stopped strutting down the corridor and stared at this dark-skinned anomaly extending a hand towards me. I'd been walking along in a daze, mentally listing all the things I was going to achieve that year:

1 Buy hip-hop records
2 Play a gig to my peers
3 Get Pentil and BS to stop taking the piss out of my surname
4 Convince my mum and dad music was a viable career choice
5 Maintain grades (I still had exam success pressure loitering in my brain)

Startled, I extended my hand to this 'Ahmed' when . . .

'Hi, I'm Jasel.'

I turned to find yet another dark-skinned anomaly belatedly arriving on the scene. They were both posh, well-spoken, tall and darker than me with raven pupils bulging out of alabaster eyeballs. What the what? Who were these interlopers? I reassessed my high-pitched surprised voice and nodded upwards, quickly, once.

'Alright.'

'Amit is it?' asked Ahmed earnestly.

'Yeah. Safe.'

'We were told to look for you,' he said. 'It's our first day.'

'Yeah?'

'I guess they think we should all stick together, eh?' quipped Jasel.

'Yeah,' I replied, not sure how to talk to these guys.

'I heard there were two other Asian guys?' Ahmed asked.

'Anand and Nishant. They're my spars.'

'I dunno why the headmaster felt the need to tell me that there were three Asians in the school,' said Jasel. 'I guess he thought I'd feel alone.'

'Sounds straight racist to me,' jeered Ahmed.

'Yeah,' I sneered. 'Sorry, who you be then?'

'Amit! Amit! Guess what?' Nishant came bounding down the corridor, looking a little distressed. 'They've moved Anand and me to another class. They've split our year into two classes cos there's so many new joiners. They wanted you to be with some new Asian guys or something and Anand and me to be in a separate class to spread us all around a bit.' He looked up and saw Ahmed and Jasel. 'Oh hi, I'm Nishant. Who are you guys then?'

'Jasel.'

'Ahmed.'

'We're the new Asians.'

'Right. OK, lovely, thanks.' Nishant waved his hands in the air and ran off.

I needed to rescue the situation.

'We're in a band actually.'

'Really?' said Ahmed 'A band? What kinda music?'

'Hip-hop.' I walked into the classroom, letting the revelation hang in the air.

'I love hip-hop,' Ahmed continued, following me. 'You know, like, Wu Tang Clan.'

I sneered again. Who was Wu Tang Clan? They weren't in my notebook of rap band names . . .

The first day of school was one of newness, of portentous talk about our exams and how we had to now grow up. As a class, we veered between being immature about work-related things and really grown up about socialising. Classmates were starting to discover booze and boobs.

I was anxious about exposing myself to alcohol, cigarettes and weed and so, despite not being invited anyway, I made up excuses about never attending weekend parties, which happened every week without fail. I was a) worried about messing up my vocals if I smoked and b) allergic to alcohol, thus unable to partake in shifty vodkas during lunchtime. It all went on down by the lake. I just tried my hardest to take the stoic approach, like I was above it but not in a judgemental way, just with a *I don't need it* kind of vibe.

I used to fear going out in the evenings without a clear exit strategy. I always needed to know how I was going to get home from anything I went to, whether through being picked up by my mum or taking the train. Whenever I left for school, with Dad who worked nearby, I would wake up my sleeping mum and tell her what time I needed picking up from school. Some days I'd get so paranoid I hadn't told her or it hadn't registered that I'd come up with an excuse to phone her from the public telephone in school, just to confirm the time. I was a homebody desperate to escape. I didn't trust the freedom of the train fully because I was too used to my parents' insistence on picking me up and dropping me off, as Dad's office was so close. I could've walked. Anand and Nishant, living near each other and half way between me and school, walked together. We'd drive past them most mornings and they'd decline lifts, set on having fun without me.

'What's the school like?' asked Jasel, penetrating my internal monologue and the resulting awkward silence.

'Some of the teachers, you know . . . ' I made the international symbol for 'wanker'. They laughed. 'Some are alright, some can be idiots, some are just . . . wankers.' They laughed again. I was too smooth for lube.

I pushed the door and entered the classroom. The boys were

already here, playing a version of cricket and football we called 'crickball'. You bowled a tennis ball underarm to the wicket – the rubbish bin – and the batsman used his foot as a bat to score runs. If you hit the back wall, you got four or six depending on bounces. If you hit the side walls you got one or two, again depending on the bounces. The game usually broke something that then had to be concealed or swapped with an adjacent empty classroom, but it was our world-beating sport and we even had a league for it. The inaugural match of the school year had Pentil at the crease. They all stopped the game to see who was coming in. It was me and my new pals, Ahmed and Jasel.

'Lads,' Pentil stopped and declared loudly, his *Where's Wally* glasses and combed forward brown hair out of step with his revered place in the school's hierarchy. 'Looks like we're having curry tonight.'

Everyone laughed.

'Wankers,' I murmured to Ahmed and Jasel.

'You swear a lot,' said Jasel.

'Well, they are aren't they?'

'Yeah, I guess. You just don't need to try and be a bad man.'

'Whatever, cuz.'

I wasn't sure what came over me. I never swore and saw it as the easy way out; I had the gift of gab, the power of lyrics – why did I need to swear?

We sat and waited for quiet to descend on the classroom. Mr Overton, our form tutor, was a machine. He was a rugby man who taught chemistry and ran on military precision. He arrived at the classroom at 8.42 a.m. every morning, giving him three minutes to arrange his things, settle the class down, find a pen and start registration at exactly 8.45 a.m. The clockwork man held our attention, not out of respect but because we were all scared of him.

He was known throughout school as 'BS' because, when he taught, he did so with the speed of an auctioneer, the unevolved grunts of a Cro-Magnon Man and the texture of processed cheese. He was a speed-lecturer, unwilling to fill in gaps if you stopped him to ask a question, almost as if he was an actor delivering carefully rehearsed monologues. He had grey eyes, cold and private school-clinical, mousing about above a mouth turned into a constant thin-lipped 'o' with the bottom lip slightly jutting out, collating all the drool. He was built for rugby, barrel-chested with meaty fingers, nails looking like they'd hardened and wrapped round his tips, like horseshoes, lacking the sensation of touch required for a functioning human sense.

It was 8.42 a.m. The tennis ball was placed in a bag. My classmates all settled down. They gave the table we'd taken up a wide berth, nodding at me and my new friends and giggling to people beyond our periphery, all caught in some private joke we weren't privy to, whispering 'pop–pop–pop–poppodom' to us as they settled.

Mr Overton entered. 'Another year I suppose,' he announced, staring his desk, not making eye contact with any of us. 'Who's been training?'

Hands went up.

'Training for what?' whispered Ahmed. I shrugged. I assumed rugby but he wasn't consistent enough with his reference points for me to be sure.

'Who can run 10k in an hour?'

Hands stayed up. I hesitantly offered my hand. BS zoned in on me like a torpedo captain.

'You? You can run 10k?' My classmates laughed.

'Yes, Sir.'

'Remind me of your name. It's gone . . . it's unpronounceable.'

'Amit.'

'Ahh, yes, Amit. Didn't I give you a better name last year? What was it? Oh damn oh fumble oh bum oh fudge oh balls what was it?'

'Chuckles, Sir!' shouted Pentil.

'That's the bajingo. Chuckles. Yes, a particularly gormless child

46

you were last year. Have you managed to develop any facial expressions for the start of term? Aren't your people supposed to be smiley?'

My cheeks burned.

'Well, Chuckles, it would appear you haven't. Now, let's get to the bottom of this. You can run 10k in an hour?'

'Sir, I was training all summer . . . '

'What for?'

'The . . . erm . . . cricket team.'

'Cricket is two terms away, Chuckles, don't lie.'

'Well, that way I'll be ready . . . '

'Right, lunchtime is an hour long, you can show me. I've got a watch that measures distance. We'll go for a run together. Keep up.'

The class was in hysterics as the swagger dripped out of me. I saw Jasel mentally deducting *pretty cool* points and sat silent, my cheeks glimmering – the familiar uncomfortable burn of school now returned.

'Is he joking?' Ahmed whispered to Jasel.

BS exploded, storming over and getting in Ahmed's face.

'Got something to say have you? What if I made you write down everything you say for the next two days, 24 hours a day, including what you say to your mother and your sister and your seventeen thousand cousins living in the same house, and you present that to me instead of lines . . . do you think you'll still have something to say?'

I could see Ahmed's eyes flicking over to me, asking if the guy was joking or not – if someone's threatening to curb your talking, do you answer them verbally when they ask a potentially rhetorical question? I squinted as if to say, 'Shut up or I'm running/you're writing and this is officially the worst day ever.' Oh to be sixteen, I thought – in two years' time the respect balance was surely due to shift.

'I thought not. By the way, who the hell are you and why are you in my class? I thought you were that Anandy Pandy pudding

47

and pie for a second. I got confused. Similar . . . err . . . eyes.'

'You mean we all look alike, Sir?' said Jasel, clearly and confidently. The class remained schtum, waiting for a new BS explosion. BS paused.

'What now? Another one? Wow, a good day for you Chuckles. Cousins of yours? Sister's uncle's brother's cousin's wife's goat's dad's boyfriends?'

'Racist,' Ahmed murmured. These kids had guts; I had nothing. I was waiting for the storm to pass, trying to make myself as invisible as possible, hoping for a klaxon to sound announcing it was time to reapply our focuses elsewhere. Please.

'I'm going to pretend, seeing as it's your first day and we're yet to be properly introduced, that I didn't hear that.' BS returned to his desk and started running through the register.

I needed to know but was afraid to ask, was I meant to be running with BS at lunchtime or not?

*   *   *

I excelled in Latin. This was always the sticking point of hilarity for my cousins and the Harrow lot. Not only was my school so posh that it taught Latin, I was posh enough to be good at it. I found languages easy, sciences hard, and it was amusing to them that I could conjugate *amo amas amat amamus amatis amant* without breaking a sweat. Even the white kids thought it was weird I was good at a subject that would have no bearing on any of our lives. It was a private school formality, but the one place I shined. I was the king of this classroom. Anand and Nishant had now been relegated to the dumber stream of classes, the reason being that they weren't even clever enough to do Latin.

Mr Pi, our Latin teacher, was a strange, small man. Two years ago, he was a bubble of fear and animosity that erupted in quiet controlled rage. Then, he fell off a curb and banged his head, and had since developed a series of comedic ticks and unconscious jerks. He wore pince-nez glasses, had thin stringy hair and an

48

overbite that made his mouth quiver unpredictably. Since the fall, if a wrong answer was given, he'd slowly approach the boy in question, place his hands on the desk, pull his face in and whisper slowly while a smile pleated itself over his top lip, 'This is incorrect, boy. Have you fecal matter for grey matter?'

We entered his classroom.

'Is this guy a . . . too?' said Jasel, miming the 'wanker' sign.

I sat next to Pentil, a boy who antagonised me so much Mr Pi thought it only fair to pair us up in an effort to build peace and harmony. We'd play this drawing game on our exercise books called 'Bash the Brown Boy'. He was 'bash the brown boy' and I was 'save the brown boy'. We'd start with a drawing of me, usually a stick figure with a name-badge that said 'Amit', and he'd draw a way to kill me, like a knife or a bazooka, and I'd have to draw a way to save myself, like a metal plate or a decoy 'Amit'.

It was the only time we were in harmony. Pentil and I had a fractious relationship, developed from the moment I was daubed 'Chuckles'. He found any opportunity for name-manipulation hilarious, but felt uncomfortable by my difference. He was ambivalent to Anand and Nishant, who were under the radar, not having any classes with him, but he had to face me every day. The race thing was my weak spot, therefore his easiest way to get to me. He had the run of the class, being everyone's go-to guy for goals, snide comments and stories about girls. I couldn't penetrate any deeper into his persona to know if he had absent dad issues or a perfectionist mum, but he wasn't clever, he wasn't interested and he wasn't willing to let me slip into the solitude of being ignored.

He was a familiar sight around the school, and had a cocky ability to make entire corridors of students gravitate to him. Pentil was popular opinion personified and made it his business to enforce his views throughout the school. As a popular strand of his annoyance I would bear the brunt of antagonism, but because this was a private school and not the urban sprawl of Harrow's rougher edges, it was only sarcasm and never physical threat.

Because I knew some dodgy people from Harrow, I thought, I believed that I was edgier than these posh wastemen and they'd suffer if it came down to the wire – but I made the mistake of assuming they wouldn't have the arms to prop up the words. In my eyes, sarcasm was a rich man's boxing glove, and I was from the streets.

I knew there was no physical threat in playing 'Bash the Brown Boy', though. Plus it was Latin, and that was my house.

* * *

Ahmed and I were walking to lunch, while Jasel was hanging behind with Pentil to talk about the rugby team, bonding over sports.

Ahmed nudged me. 'So, who's your favourite rapper?'

'Nas,' I replied without a misstep, even though I hadn't actually heard anything by Nas.

'Yeah, he's good.' Good? Just good? The guy was the best. Apparently. 'But I prefer Wu Tang . . . ' This was getting confusing now, balancing popular opinion with genuine thoughts.

'Yeah, they're alright.'

'Alright? Nas is just one man and there's about nine of them, all with skills as big as his. Mans are great. Come round. I'll play you "Protec Ya Nec". It's their gang mentality single.'

'Yeah alright.'

I said 'yes' without really thinking it'd happen. It was Thursday and I had to go to Nishant's house to listen to the radio rap show on Kiss, and hear this song by Nas everyone was talking about. Plus, I wasn't sure about this Ahmed guy yet.

My sister and I were funny about leaving our homes. We had to go to places we were both comfortable with. She refused to stay the night anywhere other than her house, but I could stay over at a house I was familiar with. Because of my weirdness of needing exit strategies and needing to know how I'd make it home, though, I found it hard going to new peoples' houses. This was starting to dissipate, the more I was mobile on public transport. But because Mum and Dad worked seven days a week to afford my school, we were left for large periods of time at home by ourselves and this meant our house became our fortress, our place of comfort and joy.

'Actually, you know what? I'm busy tonight. Can you dub it for me?'

A pause.

'I'll try. I can't do vinyl to tape at the moment . . . '

'You got Wu Tang on vinyl?'

'Yeah, course, that's how all the good shit's heard, no?'

Jasel approached us, giggling as Pentil walked away with his smug face tattoo.

'Yo Amit,' he said loudly for everyone to hear. 'I heard you've never kissed a girl!'

'What? What you chatting 'bout?'

'*What you chattin 'bout?*' he mimicked. 'You do know you go to private school . . . *blud.* Pentil told me you've never kissed a girl and I'm going to make it a personal project of mine to ensure this changes very soon. We can't have this, no no . . . '

I smiled, embarrassed. 'Whatever man. I don't even need to defend myself.'

'Don't worry my man, I'll get the goods for you.'

He walked away, taking Ahmed with him. Jasel turned around and blew me a kiss, erupting in laughter.

So what if it was true? I lived for my art. The girls would come.

I ran to room 5b, an empty classroom in an unobtrusive part of school and my usual lunchtime rendezvous place with Anand and Nishant. I was ten minutes late and they were wondering why. I was always first. I shushed them both with an enigmatic shrug and led them back to the lunch hall.

My cheeks burning, my fortress crumbling, I was shaking with the nervous energy of someone who'd never been kissed.

Next: Dope on Plastic

CHAPTER THREE

Diggin' in the Crates

'Vhy do you vaste money on CD and book? Ve liwe in England, they hawe radio and they hawe library, both free. You spend £7 on album and £5 on book. You listen to album till tape breaks and you read book only vonce. Vaste of money.'

My mum was berating me while I prepared Dad's sandwiches for work.

'That's what CDs are for, Mum. They never wear out.'

'Vhy must you alvays argue? Ve brought you up here for good schools. Don't forget you are not English. You don't talk to me like I am English mother of yours.'

'Whatever,' I muttered under my breath.

Mum would monitor on a weekly basis how many tapes appeared on my shelf, trotting this speech out whenever she noticed a significant increase.

Dad, meanwhile, had loads of cassette tapes, stacks of them, all piled up next to his drinks cabinet, which consisted of a bottle of Safeway's-own brand vodka, a bottle of Safeway's-own brand whiskey and a bottle of nice whiskey, which went untouched unless guests were over. His tapes were a source of pride, despite being mostly unlistened to. They were nearly all once-blank C-90 and C-60 tapes, filled with songs recorded from the radio, topped and tailed by DJ announcements, or copies of albums friends and family had bought that he insisted they bring over whenever they visited so he could copy them. Once arrangements for a visit had been made by my mum, she'd pass the phone to Dad who'd run through latest releases and acquisitions of new Bollywood sound-tracks and 80s disco compilations with his equivalent male on the other end, and they'd decide which ones to tape for each other. It was like when we'd collect and swap football stickers for our Panini albums, but more labour-intensive in terms of getting three or four albums copied in the time it took to visit or be visited, half an ear on another conversation about cricket and half an ear on the tape player for whether it was time to tape the next side or not. Dad's biggest pet peeve was receiving dubbed tapes from friends who'd recorded side A on one side and side B on the other, often leaving 10–20 minutes of blank tape at the end. What a waste of audio real estate.

My parents didn't discourage me from listening to music. They were happy for me to listen to whatever I wanted if it was Michael Jackson or the Beatles or, most preferably, bhangra, until hip-hop ruined my life and my innocence in their eyes. They just insisted on being frugal in the music's procurement. In a funny way, they were the first generation of audio pirates.

Dad's reaction to my tape collection was different to Mum's.

'Why have you started dressing like unstylish black man?' he'd say. 'This baggy jean is terrible contribution to fashion. Now jazz . . . they had style.' Dad did not own any jazz.

While Mum, on opening my bedroom door while I was in the middle of rapping along to 'Pain' by Tupac, 'Did someone just say motherfucker?' The word 'motherfucker' does not feature in that song.

Even my uncle had attempted to influence my musical choices. On hearing me sneaking his copy of *Absolutely Madness* upstairs so I could listen to 'Baggy Trousers', he knocked on my door and handed me a C-60 labelled 'The Specials'. He said, 'If you like Madness, listen to this. Listen to "Ghost Town", it'll change your life.' It didn't. I was nine.

My uncle left his tapes when he moved out of Dad's house and the remnants included a lot of soul and funk, like Curtis Mayfield and James Brown, whose samples I recognised from what I was listening to. Being a rap purist, celebrating the originators, I procured all his tapes to sit nicely next to my C-60 versions of De La Soul, Ice Cube, DJ Jazzy Jeff and the Fresh Prince and that annually-re-dubbed-on-to-a-fresh-tape copy of 'Rap Trax!' – a relic to Neel's listening past. (Neel had by then moved on to The Beatles and novelty comedy songs.) I left behind my uncle's punk and rock stuff, embarrassed that my dad's brother listened to white man music. I was so insensitive I'd wholeheartedly taken myself to be politically black and oppressed. He had stuff by the Clash, the Ramones, the Velvet Underground, Marc Bolan, the Specials – all bands that I love now – but I decided they had no relevance to my life because I assumed them soulless. I stuck to James Brown and Curtis Mayfield and rescued them from being pushed to the back of my dad's tape shelves, unloved and dusty.

Mum, obviously scorned by the growing number of tapes on my shelf, scoffed, not realising they were immigrants from the oppressive unlistened-to regime downstairs.

*　　*　　*

Today was the day. We were finally going to buy some vinyl and start using Nishant's Dad's dusty record player as a force for good.

The only place I knew that sold vinyl in the area was Naked Records, next to Harrow-on-the-Hill station, in a strip of un-assuming shops selling 24-hour alcoholic beverages and mis-cellaneous provisions, greasy breakfasts and light fittings.

Having saved up for a month through pocket money, presents and working for my dad in his warehouse on Sundays packing orders, we had enough for what I figured would be an impressive virgin haul. I had no idea how much records cost and could only store them at Nishant's house as my mum would balk at my purchasing more music, especially in an outdated format, which to her was even worse than spending money on CDs. Anand's mum thought hip-hop was the music of the devil, specifically the black devil. She was a little racist – literally, she was four-foot-ten – but we never dared argue with her because she had a ferocious temper and made the most buttery parathas in the county.

We headed to Harrow to hit Naked Records before our obligatory Saturday night of study, as was our boon in life. Both my mum and Anand's had insisted that we use the time when 'your Christian classmates will be out drinking and partying' to study and get ahead. Nishant's mum was taking him to the theatre in London to see a one man play about Michael Jackson's early years in the Jackson 5. His family always did fun things together.

'Blur, man, I don't get that shit,' said Anand, in case there were any doubts as to his musical loyalty as we strut-strode towards St George's Shopping Centre. 'All they do is shout in rhythm over beats and boring guitars. So what? Boring! Next . . . '

'That's rap too, innit?' asked Nishant.

'Well, people at school have no taste. They listen to all that whining jingle jangle bingle bangle stuff,' I said, backing Anand up.

'It's so white boy,' affirmed Anand.

'So gora . . . '

Saying 'gora' was our way of asserting bits of our culture we liked over our white peers, excluding *them* for a change. We pepper-sprayed our conversations with words like gora, our slang Guj-glish, words unnecessarily placed in sentences for cultural emphasis rather than syntactical rhythm.

TOP 5 WORDS IN GUJ-GLISH

1 Gora: white person/white boy (with 'gori' being the female equivalent). It was usually used in derision to white culture, as in, 'Why do white people always put raisins in their curries? Loser goras . . . '

2 Ek dum first class: really number one yes I agree. To say it properly, you need to garble saying 'first class' till it doesn't sound like English anymore – like 'furrrrssklarse'. The ek (one) DUM (pound of a bass drum) adds the emphasis, and

you need to stress DUM, like it's a sound in the background. If you're feeling particularly chipper, or you really like something and someone asked you how you were or what you thought of that thing you really liked, your chipper answer would be, 'Ek DUM furrrrssssklarse.'

3 Pendoo: culturally backward. A village idiot or someone with learning difficulties who hasn't been diagnosed with special educational needs, maybe someone from a small village high up in the Hindu Kush or on the coast in a backwater town in Uttar Pradesh, would be called a 'pendoo'.

4 Bhai: this simply means brother but we were aware of how people in hip-hop referred to each other as 'homie' or 'bro' or 'bruv' or 'homeboy' or 'brother' or 'cuz' – so this was our equivalent, customised to be culturally relevant to us despite the old hip-hop maxim that 'it isn't where you're from, it's where you're at'. So, it became the greeting of choice of affection. 'Wassup bhai.'

5 Chumchee: spoon. When we were at school, there was an annoying habit of assuming anyone who spent a lot of time with another pupil meant they were being gay together. This was a boys' school after all. Thus, if you spent a lot of time with one person, you were daubed with the title 'bum-chum'. We got it all the time: 'Amit, Anand and Nishant are such bum-chums.' Chumchee was the nice version of this. We had this thing as a perceived oppressed victimised race of the Empire – the British, not intergalactic Star Wars – an ethnic race that was kept down by the man, usually white, that we wished to not kick downwards to other races or minorities like the gay community or the disabled or even women, despite all the bitches and hoes in hip-hop. So we used the Gujarati idiom 'chumchee' to describe the idea of a bum-chum by declaring that, if two or three people always did stuff together, they were spoons. 'That Amit, Anand and Nishant are such chumchees.'

Now, here are all of these phrases in one handy conversation . . .

Me: 'Wassup bhai, you cool?'

Anand: 'Ek DUM first class bhai, you?'

Me: 'Yeah, bhai cool, just vex with Nishant.'

Anand: 'Why? What did that pendoo do now?'

Me: 'Just hanging out with that gora Richard Harvey like a chumchee.'

Anand: 'Ek DUM third class.'

We headed out of the shopping centre along the pedestrianised high street, boasting brands that meant nothing to us, the logos of the middle-class suburbanites. There was nothing for me here, something I mentally told myself every time I walked through Harrow. I had my sights set elsewhere, in London.

At the end of the high street, we turned right up to where the Fat Controller was – the pub of choice for underage drinking, two doors down from the mysterious and dank Naked Records.

Naked Records sold hip-hop vinyl. They claimed to be hip-hop and jungle specialists on the sign in a smaller font underneath 'Naked Records'. ('Naked' was written in that generic handwritten graffiti font associated with one of the four elements of hip-hop.) The grills were down so you had to stop and look through them to see what latest releases were in the window. It gave the shop a permanently closed/slightly edgy/underground feel. All signs pointed to the holy hip-hop grail, the vinyl crates.

I pushed the door open and it squelched 'JUNGLIST MASSIVE' instead of a standard bee-bop customer warning. Heavy pressure breakneck jungle was aggressively speeding out of the two khaki green spray-painted Anand-high speakers next to the door at 200 bpm. Snare-snare-snare clattering into the rafters of the shop, distorted elongated bassline choruses juddering like a helicopter attack during the Vietnam war and heavy heavy dutty dutty toasting, yah man, ins–iiiiide the DJ.

Dis a-di mixology, come wit me
Junglist massive, bassline heavy
[comeincomeincomeincomein————]

It was so aggressive, so violent and so earth-shakingly fast, all three of us recoiled in unison.

Nishant was the first to recover, unflappable in most situations due to his laid-back fuzziness. He passed me to form the deadly point of our arrow formation and walked into the shop, stickers all at angles and mish-mashed, some covering others, thrown on and shambolic, advertising legendary raves, happenings, shindigs, ciphers, bashments, record release parties and illegal warehouse parties. It was the history of urban music in the UK in the early 90s; none of it meant anything to me. They advertised SHY FX, UK APACHE, JUNGLIST, GANJA KRU. I was lost. The records were in two racks in the centre of the room like a monument to vinyl bassline culture. The steel racks were doused with stickers advertising bands and groups and MCs and graff tags, each fighting for space.

Two black guys, both wearing sunglasses in the dimly lit shop, were the only people in there. They were behind the counter, entertaining themselves with the turntables, practising DJ sets by seamlessly beat-matching new jungle tunes in every two minutes to see how they flowed. I watched them, hypnotised; it was like the beats were weapons and they had itchy trigger fingers. Nishant strode up to them and waited at the counter to catch their attention. Both the DJs were dressed in olive green khaki, with the ebony glow of their skin glinting with sweat – it was hot in the shop, and loud, the frenzy of the music adding a heavier air to the room. They both had greying dreadlocks spilling out onto the floor. One of them looked up at Nishant, his gold front two teeth gleaming and pursed into the coitus interruptus of a heavy bass-line beat-match session.

'Wha gwarn . . . ' the non-mixing DJ hoozed.

'Got any Lords of the Underground?' Nishant yelled unnecessarily, causing the other DJ to look up from cuing a record and suck his teeth, before mixing in some General Levy.

'Lords of the what-now?' The gold-toothed DJ dropped the patois and spoke in an irritated London brogue, his head darting back to the decks, knowing he was about to miss his turn on the next beat-match.

'Lords . . . of the . . . Underground,' Nishant enunciated, laying down his private school education in the form of diction.

'What kinda bam is that?'

'Bam? What's bam?' said Nishant.

'Bam . . . boom-bap . . .' he replied through sucked teeth. 'The sound of the drum. What kinda styles is dis Lord of the Underground bringing . . . ?'

'It's *Lords* – I'm sure there's more than one of them . . .' Nishant repeated, insistent.

'Whatever, bruv.' He looked like he was losing interest.

'It's hip-hop!' I blurted out, interjecting and conscious that this was actually the first ever black guy I'd directly spoken to.

'Hip-hop?' the gold-toothed one at the decks snorted.

'Pop-hop,' guffawed his deejaying friend. They laughed. The DJ at the mixer turned the faders off. The jungle stopped, replaced with the hiss of speakers, the silence of awkwardness. 'We only got mostly jungle, bruv. Try London innit.'

'What hip-hop do you have?' Nishant ploughed on. They both pointed to the racks behind us.

The faders went back up, the music spluttered to attention. Anand was rigid with fear at the prospect of talking to black people. He jumped to the racks and started filing through unfamiliar names. I joined him while Nishant remained at the counter. I watched him, embarrassed.

'What's this one called?' he asked the DJs, pointing at the speakers.

'Bad int it?' said Goldie.

'Yeah it is. Sorry . . . is that the name of the song? "Bad In Tit"?'

Meanwhile, Anand and I had sourced five potential records we assumed could only be hip-hop, despite not knowing any of the names.

Del B *Big Bad City*
MC Two Bit Trick *Pussy Love My Two Bit Trick*
Street Food *Fufu DooDoo Disco Voodoo*

Despite these not being in my notebook of rapper names, my reasoning for picking them out was simple. Del B had, like most rappers at this time, an initial in his name and did a song about a city that was big and bad and therefore ghetto, so he was probably urban. MC Two Bit Trick did a song about sex and his moniker was obviously a metaphor for his schlong, which was very much the schtick of 2Live Crew and their brand of vulgarity, so it probably stood to reason that he was a rapper too. Fufu DooDoo Disco Voodoo did a whole EP about the streets and they were probably big bad streets in a big bad city, possibly the same big bad city as Del B – which city, we couldn't be sure, but the cover artwork featured somewhere with a lot of concrete.

These were our best bets but none had the validation of a mention in *The Source* or *Hip-Hop Connection* and so were probably duff or potentially not hip-hop, and Anand and I definitely didn't want to waste our money on potentially rubbish records. We finished our intense selection in silence, not really discussing why we thought the ones we kept out could be hip-hop, just making the same jumps and leaps and assumptions in our heads. I turned to Nishant who was still standing awkwardly at the counter trying to nod in time to the furious jungle, unable to keep up.

'What's the guy so angry about?' he asked the DJs when a jungle MC started chanting '*murda-murda-murda-murderaaa SHUNNN*'.

'Dangerous,' I called, flushing under my melanin. 'We out.'

Outside the shop I stared at the sign zoning in on the lie: hip-hop specialists.

'Well that was a disaster,' I snorted.

'Yeah, true-say, bhai,' Anand agreed, leaning against the grill, one leg up, his hands in his pockets like he was the Fonz.

'Harrow sucks, man. We need to get to London.' I was getting desperate.

'Or just go to Jamming with Edwards.'

We both turned to Nishant, who was still bopping his head to the muffled beats on the other side of the shop door.

'Who-what-now?' I said.

'Oh you don't know?' Nishant replied, surprised. 'It's this record shop right next to my mum's work. I go in there a lot after school. They have loads of hip-hop.'

I stared at him incredulously. Anand shook his head, smiling.

'Wait,' I said. 'You knew there was another record shop in Harrow and kept quiet about it?'

'Yeah, I thought you knew about it. You're always in Harrow, thought maybe you'd seen it . . . '

Anand sucked his teeth at him. He'd been practising since seeing a guy do it in a film, a gangsta from the ghetto, so developed an accidental nervous habit of sucking his teeth just to get it right. It didn't sound Jamaican yet but it was getting there. Nishant's protestations of innocence faded out and he glared at his best friend, taking sides with me over him. He was hurt. You could always tell because his hands balled into fists in his pockets, his knees vibrating in frustration.

'Jamming with Edwards?' I turned to Nishant, smiling, trying to rescue the mission. Study time was looming and I needed something in the win column.

'Jamming with Edwards,' Nishant confirmed, smiling that he was back in, and it was once again his superior knowledge that would lead us to vinyl redemption.

He was still fuming with Anand, though, keeping one balled fist in his pocket while using the other to daps me on my clenched fist. He was used to my irritation and any annoyance I had with him was short-lived. His inherent good nature trumped the goofiness.

'Oh yeah, I guess I'll be leading the way then.'

He walked on, I followed, Anand slinked behind slightly slower, waiting for Nishant's balled fist to emerge from his pocket. It stayed there as we approached Jamming with Edwards. The wares advertised were diametrically opposed to the spirit of hip-hop. Each record a black horned representation of metal, with monikers like SLAYER MEGADEATH BLACK SABBATH, emblazoned with visions of hell. This was what all the extreme, disenfranchised rich kids in our school, the ones who rebelled against grunge and Britpop listened to – it was white boy rebel music.

Anand stopped. Nishant pushing open the door.

'You . . . err . . . sure this place . . . err . . . isn't it, like . . . weird?'

'Does it sell hip-hop?' I implored.

Nishant shrugged, a knowing smile across his lips, and opened the door allowing crunching distorted guitars and yell-wailing (or 'yailing') to escape and blast us in the face.

'Nishant!' an excited exclamation was exhumed from the bowels of the shop. 'How's that rap band?'

'All good Eddy!' he replied.

Anand and I exchanged 'what-the-what?' looks. A greying man with a long speckled plait of hair, a full beard, tattooed fingers and wisening pince-nez glasses looked up from a record he was cleaning with a small nail brush. Heavy metal continued to HUHURSH DUHFOOSHDH in the background tunelessly. The walls were festooned with rare records from the Beatles, Elvis, AC/DC, James Brown, Marvin Gaye and Grandmaster Flash – the originator of hip-hop no less – up there on the heavy metal tattoo man's wall. I poked Anand and pointed at it. Anand bit his lip in tacit agreement. Nishant was on to something.

'Ahh,' Eddy said warmly, laughing to himself, 'you finally brought in your band mates . . . '

'I did Eddy. They moaned, though. They couldn't believe you'd sell stuff like Tupac and Snoop just cos you have all that heavy metal stuff in your window.'

'Well,' he said, looking over his pince-nez glasses at Anand and me, 'you boys would be surprised how much of that stuff sells to the disaffected suburban disenfranchised white youth with a middle class amount of pocket money in his wallet. I'm a Beatles man myself but I've got to make my money somehow and, face it, suburban school children love goth and heavy metal – it's like a club. Tuneless, I'd say. Not like Lennon. He was the last of the greats. So you guys are the band, eh?'

'Yeah this is Amit, Mit Dogg – he's the main rapper – and this is Anand, MC AP. He's the hype man.'

'Ahh, Harrow's very own Chuck D and Flava Flav!'

'You know Public Enemy?' I asked, reticent, amazed.

'I don't *just* listen to the Beatles. I listen to everything that comes in here, everything in the papers kids'll wanna buy and everything that intrigues me. So what you guys after? You know, hip-hop-wise? I'll see what I can pull out.'

'Instrumentals,' Anand blurted out. He was excited. We were finally getting somewhere. We didn't have to invent an intricate web of lies to get to London to buy records. Not that we knew where to start, of course.

'What kinda bam?' he replied.

'Yeah, you know, usual ting,' I said, ice cold smooth. No one was gonna phase me despite my delirious happiness at finding someone who knew who Public Enemy was. 'Tupac, Snoop, Public Enemy – if you got any – that kinda ting, ya knaaa?' I'd taken to speaking out the side of my mouth. This way I sounded a bit more council estate.

'And any Lords of the Underground too.' Nishant was adamant.

'What about Lord Finesse, Large Professor, Biz Markie – you heard of these guys? That sort of stuff intrigue you? Any electro?'

'Yeah, yeah, Biz Markie's a-iiight, pull that ting out if you got it.' Who was Biz Markie?

'Well,' he pointed to a rack gloriously labelled *HIP-HOP / RAP*, 'why don't you pull out a few bits and I'll give 'em a spin here? That way you only buy *tings* you like.' He grinned.

Anand and I looked over at where he was pointing, then back at each other. Eddy had taken pity on us and our lack of knowledge/confidence and our fear of loud guitars. If not for hip-hop bravado prevailing over my public persona outside of school, where I needed to sell a reputation to the Asian kids who saw me as one of the rich boys, I would've said 'thank you' at the very least. Instead, Anand and I walked nonchalantly over to the racks and flipped through as subtly as we could, the hunger of the hunt in our eyes. We pulled out anything we'd heard of or had seen in *Hip-Hop Connection* or *The Source*, putting back the ones that didn't have instrumentals. We were left with five records a-piece.

There was a moment when the mask slipped and Anand and I burst into a two-second grin before regaining our screwfaces. I grabbed the vinyl, fluidly placing them under my arm and heading over to the counter as slowly as possible. The outward message was, 'Bruv, play me dese wax, yeah? I'll give them my time, ya get me, but I ain't in no hurry, seen?' I placed the vinyl on the counter. Eddy was making small talk with Nishant like they were old war buddies. I felt a tinge of jealousy that Nishant knew some cool old wise ninja dude with an elephantine knowledge of music and some choice records, and that he'd discovered this place over me.

Eddy scanned through the records, nodding at one or two, suggesting he approved of the choices. He looked up.

'There's a lot of that gangsta stuff in here. You don't want to try any of that boom bap stuff from New York then? Just the gangsta stuff?'

What the hell was boom bap? Luckily, in these situations it was equal parts embarrassing:helpful to have Nishant the inquisitive idiot to hand.

'What's boom bap?' he asked.

'God you don't know?' Anand exploded.

He probably knew less than I did about the scene, but he had to maintain bravado in the face of someone who knew more than us, and we were in a band and the dude was old and white so there was no possible way we could let him know he knew more about *our* scene, *our* music, *our* people, than us. Nishant, though, wasn't going to let Anand have this victory at his expense, especially as we were prostrating our feet at the bounty he'd sourced.

'No . . . explain it to me, Anand.'

Anand snorted and went back to sifting through the rest of the records. To fill the silence, Eddy took off the heavy metal records to ready his deck for the hip-hop slam-jamz listening party. The shop was silent, save for the hum of the strip lighting sound-clashing with the static crackle of old speakers awaiting their next vinyl injection.

'Seriously, Anand . . . explain it to me,' Nishant insisted. 'I would love to know. So would Amit . . . what's boom bap?'

'Tsch . . . it's like . . . whatever man . . . it's like . . . beats that go, like, boom bap-boom boom-bap . . . BOOM BAP-BOOM BOOM-BAP . . . BOOM BAP-BOOM BOOM-BAP . . . '

We giggled at Anand's flawed impression of a funky drummer 4/4 beat. Eddy pressed play and Nas dropped 'It Ain't Hard to Tell' off the stone-cold classic *Illmatic*. Our faces dropped in disbelief at the bittersweet beauty of the beat, the boyish rasp of his voice, then he said he was 'half man-half amazing'. My jaw kissed the floor.

The Nas album was high up on my list of top five albums of all time, because in the month it was released it'd received five mics (the highest honour) from *The Source* and five stars (the highest honour) from *Hip-Hop Connection*. This validation meant that I had to know about Nas. They didn't sell the album in Harrow, though, and we were pre-internet teenagers. Things acquired a mystique easily back then because you had to really seek them out. So, despite having never heard Nas utter a single word, I had him in my top five rappers and top five albums of all time, because I chose to believe the hype.

Then Richard Miles, a musophile classmate obsessed with anything the indie music press recommended, showed me a positive review of *Illmatic* in a copy of his beloved *NME* and asked if I had it.

'Of course,' I replied. 'It's one of my top five albums of all time. Haunting lyrics over funky yet broody beats.' I paraphrased a review I'd read. It had to be amazing if the *NME* liked it because they, I'd decided, hated black people like me and never spoke about bands I liked. The *NME* was straight up racist. If they were interested in a hip-hop album, it must be half man-half amazing.

'Cool,' Richard Miles replied, smiling. 'Can you tape it for me? It got an excellent review.'

I dodged him for a few months with excuses about not being able to, not having the time to, not being bothered to tape it. When I was out of sensible excuses, I played the race card and told Richard Miles straight: 'Taping the album for you is selling out to the white man, letting him have our music. Nah, man. For us by us . . . '

'But you're not black.'

'Fuck you, Miles. I'm politically black from an oppressed race. Don't speak to me about no race politics or I'll lynch you like you done to my people.'

'I'm Jewish . . . '

'Whatever man. I ain't got no tapes.'

Then the summer came, and I'd dodged him enough to hope that he'd moved on to new Oasis singles. On the first day of term, though, he'd said he'd bought it when he was in London so there was no need for me to tape it. He'd really liked it. He'd found it 'moving'.

'Yeah man, standard,' I'd said. 'It's too cool.'

'What's your favourite song?'

I reeled off the name of the one song I'd heard mentioned in the

Kiss Rap chart, but never managed to listen to. Nishant had heard it. He'd told me it had a Michael Jackson sample in it.

'That'd be "It Ain't Hard to Tell" son.'

'That's a good song but it's all bluster and bravado, no? It lacks the street politics of "The World is Yours" or the perceptive emotiveness of "One Love".'

'Whatever cracker,' was all I could manage.

Back in the shop, Nishant was delirious and vindicated, humming 'Human Nature' by Michael Jackson.

'It's got a Michael Jackson sample in it. Can you hear it?' I was deep in the mix, following the cadence of his delivery, hypnotised and unaware of what cadence was, lost in the rhythmic pain and passion of Nas and his bleak yet poetic spin on the world; a tattered notebook in his hand, face pressed up against the window of his ninth floor apartment, watching the street flow down below. It was beautiful. 'Can you hear it?' Nishant continued, singing the chorus of 'Human Nature' a little louder so we could hear and there wasn't any doubt at all.

'I want this. No, I *need* this,' said Anand.

'And the album.' I concurred.

Eddy laughed. 'I'm relieved. I always knew someone'd buy that album eventually.'

Records piled up, instrumentals were sourced and prepared, the backs of our necks ached from nodding along, cash was exchanged and we left the shop a collective £50 poorer. We headed back to Nishant's house to tap the record player and tape some of the tunes before Nishant's dad returned home to shame us by listening to his Bollywood shit and other such farted travesties to the ears. Time enough to get inspired for some rhymes and rhyming, dub the instrumentals on to tapes and head our separate ways for Saturday night: Nishant to the theatre in London with his parents; Anand to his sister's friend's sister's birthday party at Moonlightin' to try and pull girls, something he was becoming increasingly successful at; and me home to 'study' but actually read old *Spider-*

Man comics, listen to my dubs in my headphones and wait till my mum and dad went to sleep before sneaking downstairs to watch whatever film was on our late-night channels, hoping for breast-sightings.

First, though, we had a listening party and arrived back at Nishant's full of it. Auntie Naina and Tejal, his mum and sister, were out – Tejal at her cricket club and Naina at the Adult Learner's Centre for her weekend Russian classes. I loved Nishant's parents, mostly because they were proud of Nishant for being in a band, always bemoaning their immediate family's lack of musical ambition. Nishant loved hanging out with them and never went out with Anand on Saturday nights or came over to mine as, chances were, his parents had organised culturally enriching activities for him and his sister, and they were off doing exciting things in the centre of London. My parents never went out.

'Do you think we have time to make fun in the London city and party-sharty?' they'd say.

Nishant turned on the hi-fi. I got a shiver down my spine as the LED display lit up the front in a mixture of electronic dull blue-grey and orange. The robot sound-box was coming alive. Anand pulled out one of the vinyls from his TOKING record bag with fetishistic relish. I leaned on the half-size pool table, steadying myself, ready to bust out the moves and bang my head when the beat dropped. I'd planned this moment for weeks now. When that first instrumental came on, I was going to launch into a rap I'd written over the interim weeks and spent every spare moment committing to memory till it was word-perfect and rhythmically tight. I'd been waiting for this wow factor moment of simulated spontaneity, at which point I'd let rip and Coconut Unlimited would truly be born in the spirit of my apparent freestyle.

The crackle spat, the lever dropped – the pregnant loaded gun of silence – then BANG BANG BOOM-BAP BOOM BOOM-BAP. We were OFF.

I waited to come in . . . wait boom-bap not yet boom boom-bap . . . .now? Boom bap . . . no . . . boom boom-bap . . . well . . .

'Is this the instrumental?' I yelled. The boys' heads were nodding. I couldn't tell if it was to the music or my question. Sod it. I went for it.

'Hollaaaaaaaaaa!' I screamed with my gun hand in the air. The boys were shocked out of their stupor, Anand clutching his chest as if I'd jumped his bones.

> *I'm like coconut water . . .*
> *You know you outta*
> *Don't test this diss man*
> *I'll take you down to Chinataaahhhn*
> *I'm not Cockney, no no no*
> *I'm from Harrooooo, yooooo . . .*
> *Jump low, step smart, get your street smarts*
> *The beat roots hard like a retard*
> *En guarde, musketeer, gendarme*
> *Best believe I'll strong arm*
> *You – tone, cut you filleted*
> *Don't mess with Coconut Unlimited . . .*

Well, this is what should've come out of my mouth. I didn't get past 'Hollaaaaaaaaaa', which I repeated thirty seconds later just to make some noise again, before stage fright reduced me to a shadow of nerves and stuttering neuroses. 'HOLLAAAAAAAAAA!' The panic of not knowing where a drum pattern started and where I was supposed to come in, the cataclysmic unbelievable lameness of my rapping style – it was all too much.

An hour later, I walked home with a tape of instrumentals on one side and *Illmatic* on the other. I walked with a pimp strut, a lazy left leg and sagging shoulders leading the way. 'Oh yeah boys and girls,' I was telling Harrow, I got *Illmatic* the best album ever on tape and I've got a date with my tape player at home. You can't stop me, can't hold me down, can't test me now . . . ' I recited my own verse over and over again in my head, tapping my thigh with my palm to give me a tempo, speeding up and slowing down depending on the lyrics.

I had it perfectly in my head and in private, so why couldn't I say it in front of my bandmates and my best friends?

*   *   *

Arriving home, I could see the kitchen light on and Mum washing up, the window misted with condensation as the pressure cooker blew off some steam on the hob to her right. She was framed in the window, soap suds in her hair, the grimace of a woman with struggle in her hunched shoulders and tired eyes.

My bedroom light was on, meaning my sister was on the phone, which sat on a small squeaky plastic table outside my room. She was probably talking to her friends Dina or Rachna about some Bolly-wood rubbish or some Harrow boy bhangra muffin tough guy – or something else equally dreary. What a boring life she led, I thought. So insular. All her friends were Gujarati. All her references were Indian. Her entire life was a battle to be more Indian than our mum, twice removed from the country of the culture she pushed on to us both. I was headed the other way, obviously.

She needed to get out immediately; I had this tape burning a hole in my pocket, buzzing with potential. I wanted to avoid a dinner-guilt trip with my mum and kick my sister out stealthily.

Mum's way of checking my comings and goings wasn't to just ask me where I was off to. She wanted to give me the illusion of freedom now I was a teenager, but still felt it her duty to monitor how much time was spent studying and how much time being a 'ruckuryu' – which, loosely translated, means a 'messer-abouter' – so instead of asking where I was off to, she'd ask, 'Am I cooking for you tonight?' It would drive me insane.

'Stop monitoring me, Mum,' I'd say. 'Cook for me every night and I'll eat it at whatever time I'm in . . . '

'Vell, if I know, then I can keep the rotis hot for you . . . '

I wanted to avoid any such exchange, grab my headphones

and my walkman and listen to Nas. The key fell into the lock smoothly and I timed opening the door with the next blast from the pressure cooker, hissing, filling the house with the smell of starch and onions. A light emanated from the lounge door where Dad was listening to Abba and staring into space, thinking about the business. The stairs smelt like old, damp paper as the chipboard was coming away from the walls, a decorating sacrifice to the Gods of Amit's school fees.

I flipped myself into the house and up the stairs like a ninja, pressing the door closed and using the weight of my body to dampen the sound. I stealthed up the stairs, avoiding creaky step ten and the floorboard at the top that sounded like an industrial hole punch if you hit it. I pushed my door open violently, catching it quickly so it remained silent as it whacked my sister's elbow. She yelped and glared up at me, arguing with me before I'd opened my mouth to lay down my claim to the sovereign state of solitude in my room.

'If you're just listening to that gangsta rap shit, listen to it in my room. Rachna needs me.'

'Get out Nish!'

'But it's my turn on the phone, you pendoo.'

'I don't give a dutee [shit] – get out.'

'Oh look,' she said to Rachna on the phone. 'Coconut bro learned another Gujie word . . . nah.' She pressed into the mouthpiece. 'Just my bro being a prick as usual.' She picked herself up and resigned herself to leaning against my closed door, in the corridor, where she could be spotted and ordered to give up the phone and return to her room and study. Saturday night's feverish moans of unfulfilled social lives stalked the corridors of our house.

The smell of condensation, starch from the cooking rice and steamed okra in sizzling onions reached my room. Yuck, acrid okra. Mum had blatantly made my least favourite dish because she knew I wouldn't be cooking for myself and her ultimate revenge would be me eating her food and not enjoying it. She was an evil genius.

I opened my window and let the dying embers of September's Indian summer float in, grabbing my Walkman from under my pillow, jumping on my bed and kicking off my shoes. I took the tape from my pocket and slipped it into the Walkman, hitting 'play'. The cassette muffled, chewed and stopped. I panicked . . . EJECT EJECT.

What? I pulled it out. It needed rewinding, was all – for one awful moment I thought it'd succumbed to the tape Gods. I placed it in the electric tape player and rewound it, saving batteries, looking up at the poster of Nas looking stoned and bleak but superfly cool on my wall, slightly embarrassed that, six months after the poster went up, I was finally going to listen to the actual music.

The tape stopped, rewound. I was ready to be wowed. The sheer weight of expectation was electric. I mean, how were you supposed to react to an album you thought should be good, critics said you needed in your life and the likes of Richard Miles, self-professed white boys with guitars aficionado, were willing to make the crossover for? What if it was rubbish? I hovered over 'play' about to . . . KNOCK KNOCK. Mum burst in while the obligatory second knock was fading out.

My mum was small, a paunched version of a once beauty, now elasticated under hypochrondria, expanded under the laziness that went hand in hand with overwork. She worked seven days a week in three different jobs, one of them for my dad, in order to bolster up the lack of profits in his failing business. She operated under the impression that everyone was having a better time than her, all the time, but that her struggle in life through illness and paying for her son's tip-top education was far more honourable than everyone else's 'Life of Riley'. She thought it made her more humble, when in fact it gave her a feeling of martyrdom.

'Vhen did you get home?' she demanded, posing it as a question for formality's sake.

She was stern when it came to impressing on me the need for me to repay the financial investment in my education, by going to university – I'd be the first in my family – and getting a proper job like a lawyer or doctor or accountant, something other immigrants of my parents' generation were impressing on their own children who went to state comprehensives. The only difference was, I was privately educated and therefore afforded more opportunities. What those opportunities were, I had no idea, apart from a working gym, rugby teams and hearty school lunches to keep me strong and healthy. I was an above-average student, but I'd stopped trying in my efforts to disappear from view, filling my notebooks with raps and logos for Coconut Unlimited instead of notes from class. I was torn between wanting to do well for my parents, and wanting to be either accepted or comfortably ignored by my peers, until it was time to unleash Coconut Unlimited on their worlds and have them worship me as only I deserved.

'A few hours ago,' I said.

'Don't lie to me. You've been with that pendoo and that beva-koof [idiot] again, haven't you? All day you spent, not one book open. Out, being ruckurya, nah? Don't lie. Is that vhat they teach in this school ve pay all this money for?'

Mum wasn't a fan of Anand or Nishant. She thought Nishant was cute but dumb, while Anand was adversely affecting my studies and directly responsible for my growing teenage apathy. My stray into coconuttiness could be directly linked with my friendship with him. I was vehemently defensive of Anand, especially seeing as Mum was always trying to enforce her Gujarati friends' teenage male children on me in an effort to supplement my imbibing of Indian culture with more Indian faces. Or trying to get me to befriend Nish's friends' brothers as they were also all invariably Gujarati. For some reason I could never fathom as a child, she felt Anand and Nishant just weren't Indian enough for me to hang out with.

'Jeez-us, Mum, don't call them idiots, they're my best friends.'

73

'I vill call them vhat I vant dear. Dinner is ready.'

She bustled out in a tidal wave of pent-up fury and depression. I pressed 'play' and melted the next thirty-five minutes away in an oblivion of beats and rhymes.

Mum's problem with the way I lived my life was her sense that she needed everyone to see how much she struggled. While her nouveau riche brothers and sisters increased in prosperity, property, girth and tummy, our once-revered detached house shrunk and crumbled. I was her way out, a fortune in waiting because of my education, and I would lead her to well-proportioned mansions. I was her only hope.

But I was 'oondho', which means 'the wrong way around'. (It's also a colloquialism for being gay.) It all started when it was discovered I was left-handed – oondho, because this was tradition-ally the hand reserved for wiping your bum. Your right hand was for eating and writing, your left for bum-cleaning. Indian girls would paint their left hand with nail varnish so they could eat with their right, varnish-free, while the cruddy particles of poo collecting under their left hand nails would be obscured from view by red or pink varnish. Bizarrely, even my teachers at the private school attempted to get me and Adam Harvey to write with our right hands, by placing us to the right of our desk buddies so our elbows would constantly bump together, and by making us stay in the classroom one lunchtime a week practising writing with these right hands – that is, till my nosebleeds and Adam Harvey's headaches put a stop to the barbary.

Mum finally accepted I was oondho and concentrated on en-suring the rest of me would be all right.

Being left-handed was an inauspicious sign, though, and she suspected I was either headed for ruin or an underpaid job. That cushy granny flat seemed so far off because she couldn't rely on my sister to end up earning loads of money. She was state-educated.

*   *   *

Coconut is not a limited company
We're forever lasting like Hush Puppy
We go where it is sunny
I find it funny you want money
When revolution is round the corner
We're public enemies in the slaughter
We're driving round in jeeps that hum
While you still get dropped off by your mum . . .

*   *   *

'Can vee have talk pleaze?'

My internal alarm bell started ding-dinging. Dad wanting a talk usually meant Mum had been in his ear about my lack of study-time, and that I needed one of his famous pep talks to stir me into action.

'Yeah . . . '

'Come dovnstairs.'

I put my walkman down and my notepad under my pillow – nothing was sacred in this house – and then followed Dad downstairs. I slouched in a chair opposite his favourite thinking couch where he'd sit everyday from 5.30 p.m., when he returned from work, till 8.30 p.m. when his dinner was handed to him and he relocated three steps to his left to the TV-watching sofa. He'd sit on his thinking couch and stare into space, only getting up during these three hours to refill his vodka tonic or to wee his vodka tonic out.

Choice cuts from the pep talk:

1. GUILT

'Your mum tells me you are spending too much time vith that *Ahhh-nundth* [Anand] and this hip-hop and to not be studying?'

'Your mum tells me you are buying this hip-hop music vith money and not taping. How much is your fees that you have spare money for musics.'

'Vith vhat ve spend on you, ve expect A grades. Your mum tells me you are getting Bs?

2. EVALUATION OF WORKING METHODS
'You are not methodical.'

'You are not focused.'

'You like things too much. Not facts.'

3. PROPOSAL OF NEW WORKING METHODS
'You need to be more methodical.'

'You need to focus.'

'Learn more facts. Forget about things.'

4. HEART-WARMING STORY
'Vhen I was two years older than you, I vas in England penniless, so I vent to the place vhere I knew they make some money – Vembley Stadium – and I found the nearest office block next to it. I knocked on every single door and ask for job. I didn't get one but I had determination, I was methodical, I was focused on my objective.'

I couldn't help myself by this point.
'But you didn't achieve it . . . ' I said.
I went to bed that night feeling rubbish about myself, about my waste of space band and about the road of book-learning that lay ahead. I put Nas on and fell asleep to his anguish, mirroring my own dystopian (sub)urban hell on earth.

Next: Brown-Skinned Lady

CHAPTER FOUR

Girls Girls Girls Girls Girls I Do Adore

'She is so buff.'

'Bare buff . . . '

'She is tick.'

'Bare tick . . . '

'She is superfly.'

'OK!' I cried, interrupting them. 'I get it.'

I was bare vex. I was sitting with Anand and Nishant in our empty classroom at lunchtime, hearing the scuff of trainers and the bray of bored boys pounce around the corridor outside like klaxons of fury at a Public Enemy concert. Anand had missed practice, our first practice no less, because he'd been out with some girl – and he didn't seem to care. Worse still, Nishant had met her too because he'd run into them snogging on a bench behind Harrow-on-the-Hill station. I felt left out, plus Coconut Unlimited was lagging behind and I'd spent the weekend writing lyrics instead of reading *Othello* and now had an essay due. While Anand was prancing around with girls, my music career was waiting in the wings. Plus, as Nishant affirmed, she was bare nang.

'What's going on, Mit?' he asked.

'We got bare work to do. While youse two are playing up dis kissy-face business, I've been in da lab, ya get me, working . . . '

'On what, Mit?' Nishant asked, upset I was upset, sad I was sad, deflecting my fury with tenderness.

'Lyrics, bars, rhymes . . . seen?'

'Wow, wicked – can we hear them?'

'You could have, I thought . . . if Anand had been at practice.'

Only we didn't have anything to practise yet. It'd just be me trying to rap over instrumentals and Anand going 'YEEEAH' every now and then. Nishant didn't have a role to play yet except cue up the records, but the lack of a second deck for seamless mixing and matching made him an extravagant on/off button. Scratching was a long way off. All he had to do at that point was nod his head in time and not do any of his stupid dances in my periphery while I tried to concentrate.

I was jealous of Anand's pulling power. I'd been invited to go with him to this party at his sister's friend's house, but felt more comfortable being around my tapes and the looming foreboding of homework than drunk people, especially girls. Also, the party was in Wembley and there was a wishy-washy plan to get home on the last bus or maybe stay the night there. After Dad's pep talk, I had to present the illusion of a hard-working man.

The week at school had been awful. I'd gone in with a new resolve to get so good at my studies, particularly the weaker sciences, I could just coast along and do my band under the radar. But I'd forgotten to revise a particularly easy Latin con-jugation for a test and failed miserably, causing Mr Pi to keep me behind while others left, shaking their heads. 13 out of 20. Pitiful.

'13 out of 20, eh? That's pitiful.'

'I know, Sir.'

'Have you fecal matter for grey matter?'

'No, Sir.'

He leaned in close. 'Well pull up your socks boy! This is not remedial class. You are my prize and I will have you.'

'Yes, Sir.'

'Leave the room in the next thirty seconds or I will end your days.'

Pentil was waiting for me outside the room, slouching over the lockers, flicking his fringe away from his face.

'13 out of 20,' he said, shaking his head.

'What do you want?' I asked, pitched between the meek-me dealing with him in public and the assured-me dealing with him one-to-one, still stinging from my Mr Pi telling-off.

'Yo, Amit – walk with me.'

'Why?'

'I ain't gonna beat you up, you paranoid pak-o. Just walk with me.'

I went with him, knowing that we were evenly matched when it came to not being handy with our fists. We walked down the corridor to the stairs next to the loud boiler room, an explosive medley of steam bursts peppering our stilted conversation behind the walls.

'Right, Amit, where I can buy some stuff?'

'What stuff? Like, hip-hop tapes?'

'No you jungle bunny. Weed. You know guys right?'

'What makes you think I know guys?'

'Come on. Isn't your cousin Ash a dealer in Harrow? I seen him.'

'Ash ain't my cousin. He's just some ruffneck bhangra muffin from round the way. Why do you think he's my cousin?'

'Dunno. You sure you're not related? You look pretty similar.'

'Racist . . . ' I started to walk away.

'I'm no racist,' he said, grabbing my arm. 'At least I'm not a pigga. God I hate you, Amit. Actually, I don't hate you. I feel sorry for you. You just don't know who you are do you?'

'So why would you want me to help you?' I said, trying to get away again.

'I just want to buy some weed. That's all. I didn't think you were gonna make me jump through hoops for it. I'm not asking you to smoke some with me. You won't get in trouble.'

'You wanna buy off Ash, you go buy off him – I ain't stopping you,' I snarled, worried about being caught holding drugs.

'Can't you, like, introduce us or something?'

'I don't know the bredda.'

'Oh right . . . I thought you said . . . '

'I never said anything. Buy your own drugs. I don't want anything to do with it.'

I pushed past him and walked away. He tripped me and I fell into a banister. I gasped for air, trying to get my lungs to work in reverse, while Pentil smirked and walked away.

Monday set me off to a bad start.

*   *   *

'So they've got some R. Kelly playing, yeah? And everyone is bumping and grinding, cos it's "Bump'n'Grind", and my sister has left me to go and chirps Sanjay so what do I do? I start walking around the crowd, but all the lights are off and everyone is, like, pushing their hips up on each other and I'm, like, dude where's mine? So I head to the kitchen and there's no one there so I think, you know what, if I'm not gonna pull I might as well get well drunk so I open the fridge to find some beer or something and the fridge is full . . . of . . . home-cooked . . . samosas. So I'm, like, you know what? Whatevs, man needs to eat, ya get me? So I grab, like, seven of them and find a plate and heat them up in the microwave. I'm at the kitchen table while they're all dry humping next door, just eating these samosas, when this girl bursts in. She's well tick. She's, like, 16 or something, short straight hair like Lois Lane, milk chocolate skin and massive lips and glasses – you know I like my glasses, right? And she's, like, "What the hell are you doing? Those are for my mum's prayer group. You can't eat them." She goes to grab the plate and I put my hand on hers to, like, you know, stop her or something. And she looks at me. It's so hot, she's just looking up over her glasses, and she says – get this – she says, "Are they nice?" Can you believe it? "Are they nice?" You know what I say? "You know I love my cooked food darling." So then she grabs one and takes a bite and makes this noise, like this, "Mmmmmmmmmm . . . " It is so hot, man, you know? So you know what I do? I make the same noise too. "Mmmmmmmmmmm . . . " And I hold up the samosa triangle and I say, "This reminds me of eating something else." And she giggles. She knows exactly what I'm talking about. She's some sort of freak too. So she sits down and she says, "What else do you like eating?" And I'm thinking, do I joke or do I sexy? Jokey or sexy? Jokey or sexy? So you know what I do? I say, "Muff–ins." Get it? Muff–ins. And she laughs. So you know what I do next? I lean in for a kiss. I just do it. I'm a pimp, I'm a player, I'm a hustler, I'm a man, ya seen? I lean in for a kiss and she leans forward too and we're kissing and, half-way through the kissing, the samosas keep repeating on us, and she burps into my mouth and it's like this onion and garlic shit bath or something just exploded in my mouth, so I pull away and she puts her hand to her mouth. She's embarrassed and yeah it's a bit disgusting but it's only midnight and my sister's gonna be busy till 2 a.m., so I might as well keep snogging this girl, right? So I'm, like, "Nah it's cool darling. I just realised I don't even know your name." Yeah, that's right boys! I pulled this girl and I didn't even know her name. It's Meena by the way. Amazing. It was so amazing. Actually, you know what? I'm meeting her this Saturday so I can't come to Jamming with Edwards – sorry boys. Run it without me . . . '

*   *   *

Saturday. Having called off practice so Anand could hang with Meena, then gone to Jamming with Edwards to discover Eddie didn't have anything new this week, Nishant and I trudged down the high street. He was already making his excuses to leave, feeling weird at the Anand-shaped hole. I was desperately trying to fill up his silences with talk of new records that were coming out, and how I couldn't believe Anand had dumped us for his girlfriend.

'Yeah, so Mit, do you mind if I head home?' he said, interrupting my flow.

'What? We've got the whole afternoon planned.'

81

'But without Anand here, it's, like . . . what's the point?'

'Come on, man. We've got band stuff to discuss.'

'You don't need me for that. I'm in the middle of painting this new canvas of Michael. It's all I can think about. I'm going to head off. Give me a shout if Anand's free later.'

'Whatever.'

I watched Nishant hurry off, glad to be free. I was in front of St George's Shopping Centre, unsure of what to do with my day. I didn't want to go home just yet as Mum was unwell and not working today, and this meant her monitoring my movements. On a whim, I decided to do a circuit of the arcades in St George's, a big room on the first floor that housed pool tables, five bowling lanes, a zoo of big arcade games and a café that no teenager was allowed to even look at without ID. Why they'd bothered to get an alcohol licence still bothered me, but then why anyone bothered to drink alcohol in the first place also bothered me.

This was where all the Asians in Harrow's comprehensive comprehensive school system went on a Saturday. They swarmed here from thirteen-to-eighteen, with Ash as their focal point, the badboy who might sell the thirteen-year-olds porn, the fourteen-year-olds grassy weed, the fifteen-year-olds fake ID, the sixteen-year-olds grassy weed and fake ID, the seventeen-year-olds skunk and the eighteen-year-olds grassy weed when too much skunk had addled their tiny minds. It was Harrow's very own Circle of Life.

Ash was one of those creepy teenagers who always associated with people much younger than him. This was partly because his peer group had all left for universities and grown beyond Harrow, partly because he had a constant stream of teenagers to sell weed to and partly because we all feared him and his erratic temper – and fear gave him cool points in our suburb. He had a tattoo of Hanuman on his forearm, some miscellaneous Hindi scroll on his inner arm, and Shiva's face on the back of his neck. Ash always wore a baseball cap, pulled down and slightly to the side, proclaiming his allegiance to the LA Raiders. It was rumoured by the few girls unfortunate to be cajoled into having sex with him that he had 'THUG LIFE' written on his torso in some gothic script, much like Tupac, his hero.

I avoided Ash because I was scared of him. He was the closest thing to ghetto in my life, despite his uncle's successful nationwide car business, his BMW and the fact he didn't need to work for a living. The weed-selling was more of a status generator than an income maker. He had no hustle for the game. I was scared of his illegal activities, though, thinking that any association could also land me in jail.

I also avoided Ash because I was embarrassed by him. He was everything I hated about being Asian. He listened to loud bhangra in his BMW, spoke in a stupid bud-bud/street-slang hybrid accent and was only friends with Indians. He was really traditional underneath his sculpted beard and the shaved lines in his eyebrows, militant about Hindu pride, never servicing Muslim customers directly. He knew exactly who I was because you did in Harrow; of our age, we were all known to each other, and we all played a part in the social structure.

TOP FIVE ASH RUMOURS

1 He sold weed grown in Kenya and shipped over after being blessed by a guru in Mombasa port

2 His mum had been in a Bollywood film once

3 He beat up someone for leaning on his car while they were having a conversation

4 He forced someone called Roshan to sell weed for him for free because he lit up a cigarette in front of his house, causing a massive affront to his family

5 He had been to a Young Offenders Institute for getting his teacher in a headlock and threatening to bum him unless he got a B for a test

Of course, none of these rumours could be verified. They just spread, almost like they were made up for his benefit, to build up his mystique. He had to have a reason to still be living at home at twenty-two, not working, selling teenths to teenagers while holding court around a pool table in the St George's Shopping Centre arcade.

Whatever the truth of it, though, he was someone Anand, Nishant and I knew to avoid.

'Yes Amit, you cool?'

I snapped out of my daydream, realising I'd walked straight into the lion's den, and Ash was standing by the pool table in front of me, surrounded by girls.

'What's gwarnin, Ash?' I said meekly.

'What's gwarnin? You turned black overnight or something, blud? Remember your roots yeah? Ya get me? We're from a proud race of people that deal in spiritualism and enlightenment. The black man deals in guns and violence. Stay brown and proud. Safe?'

I recoiled in fear. This was the longest we'd ever spoken and he was dropping race bombs that contravened everything I believed in life and hip-hop.

'Safe, Ash.'

'Step into my office.'

I couldn't move, I was so scared. He grinned.

'You pendoo, I don't actually have an office. I just want you to walk with me and have a private chat.'

My heart was pounding, my mouth a dry mix of sand and stammer, my legs throbbing in fight-or-flight preparation. What did this notorious real-life drug dealer want with me? Was he going to push drugs on me? Turn me into a stoner? Force me to smoke weed? Get me addicted so I'd always buy it from him? I followed him in quick nervous steps, stubbing my toes repeatedly against the ground. He led me out of the arcade in silence, down the escalators to the side door where we emerged, on the main road. I was hoping no one could see me with this embarrassing drug-dealing psycho.

'You go to that posh school yeah? What them guys like over there? They friendly to you?'

'Yeah . . . '

'Good. Listen, just because you're an oppressed race in an oppressive regime, don't let them give you no shit. You go Black Hole of Calcutta on them.'

'I think the Black Hole of Calcutta was a . . . '

'Listen, history is for winners and, right now, I just see a loser.'

I stared at the ground, my voice lost in fear.

'Fucking hell, you're the pussyhole I thought you were. Patience, man. I get to the point when I get to the point ya get me? But seeing as you've asked me a question, I'm required to answer it, so here's your answer: I got a question for you.'

I looked up at him.

'Who is best placed to sell my products in your school? I ain't stupid. I know these boys got pocket money, a lot of it, and instead of them spending it on Diamond White and porn and shit, I want them to buy my weed. Do they like weed over there? Do they like rap?'

'Nah, indie,' I mumbled.

'Interesting. Sounds like the perfect music to get stoned to. Now, I need you to introduce me to someone, someone white, who can shift this product.'

'Erm . . . '

'You're probably wondering why I don't give you this task and I'll tell you why, Amit. There's a bunch of reasons. Mainly, reason A, number one, is that you're a pussyhole and you don't got the stomach or the heart or the hardness for this. Now, I'm not saying you got to have stomach or heart in life but in this you do and you don't – you're a mummy's boy. You're like my sister's mate's cousin, Sheena . . . '

'Am I?'

'Yeah, she's a pussyhole, but for different reasons you don't need to know about. Reason two B is that I don't want the stereotype of my people to be typical drug dealers.'

'But there isn't a stereotype . . . '

'Shut up. You're in a privileged position and I fully expect you to change the world, take up a position in industry, be the same as these boys out here. You got that opportunity so don't fuck it up. You're in the white man's club now, Amit, it's your duty to our people to do something with it. And don't embarrass us.'

'OK . . . '

'And reason three C. They won't trust buying weed off you. I need a face they can trust and a face that can easily be threatened by my own face, ya get me? If I get one of their own to do it, then they'll all do it. So, I want you to give me a name and a number. I'll do the rest.'

My heart was pounding. What should I do? What the hell was he talking about? What would he think about my famous band? I wanted to give him Pentil's name but I couldn't acquiesce to that just yet. I wondered if I could introduce them, if he'd do it, if he wouldn't tell on me, if I could watch Ash shit him up about not double-crossing him. I could stand there all silent, like a true thug, ya get me?

'Erm . . . '

'Look, you give it some thought but not too much thought because I'm gonna wait for you after your school lets out on Monday, and all you have to do is walk the bredda up to me and then leave.'

'OK.'

'Right, fuck off now.'

'Peace out.'

'And don't talk like a black man. Have some respect for your culture, you bitch-ass motherfucker.'

I walked away, gob-smacked that I'd entered the black arcade of Calcutta and got mixed up in Ash's business. Now I was an accessory to drug dealing at school. I could be properly done for this. Who to choose, though? Who to drop into the belly of the Ash? Well, the pocket of the Ash.

This was serious. Real serious.

*   *   *

'Did you talk to him?'

'Talk to who?' I played coy. Pentil could be wired.

'Oh come on, did you talk to Ash?'

'Yeah, I saw him round the way.'

'What's he going to do? Have you got it on you? How much do I owe you?'

'Listen, Ash ain't interested in someone copping teenths of weed off him, ya get me? He's looking for franchising. That's all I know. If you interested, I'll bring you to him, but that's all the involvement I want. I know nothing.'

'What? Like, sell weed here?'

'I didn't say nothing about weed OK, *narc*? I'm just saying, I'll introduce you. You work out the finer details. Safe?' I'd been watching cop films all weekend, paying close attention to the ones where evidence was used against the patsy who had nothing to do with nothing. I was careful now to ensure nothing I said was even vaguely incriminating.

'But he'll sell me some stuff?'

'Whatever man. I'm just introducing two people.' My heart was beating like drum'n'bass, my mind spinning like one of Terminator X's records. I was in a kerfuffle of the highest variety. This was drugs, actual proper real drugs, not the fun party-time whacky baccy that Snoop and Dre rapped about.

I walked away from Pentil, removing myself from incriminating conversation, towards the empty lunchtime classroom where I found Nishant practising a card trick involving a glass of water, a tea-towel and two decks of cards. Anand was staring blankly at his exercise book.

'Amit!' He looked up, happy to see me for the first time in days. 'I need your help.'

'What?'

'I told Meena that I'm in this band, and she kinda assumed I was the front man . . . '

'Why did she assume that?' I bounded in a cloud of passive aggressiveness.

'I told her. But she's kissing me and her hands are getting closer to my thing. Sorry but it was just between us for a little fun and play and ting. Nothing serious.'

'Right. What do you need?'

'Well, Mr Lyricist, she's kinda expecting some lyrics about her in our next song . . . '

'We haven't even got *one* song yet. You missed practice, you pendoo.'

'Yeah, well, I'm supposed to write some lyrics for her. Mind if you turn your genius to some love poetry? Like LL Cool J-style stuff?'

'Whatever.' I was all about doing favours for people today, it appeared. 'You owe me. *Practice.*'

My time to shine, I thought to myself. I could write something brilliant to show Anand and Nishant what a dope lyricist I was, but at the same time maybe throw in some oblique references to Meena's ugliness or something and make her go away. I was scribbling some ideas down in my notebook when Nishant looked up and asked if it was true I was hanging out with Ash in Harrow. I froze, my pen hovering over the word 'projectile'. Nishant told me that Jasel and Ahmed had seen me.

'Oh . . . ?' My heart burned downwards like a firework fizzling out in sodden grass. 'What? Oh no, that? Nah, that's all . . . whatever. Nothing, you know. He was just being Ash, you know. This and that. Nothing really . . . '

'Amit, be careful. The guy's dangerous. He's, like, four years older than us.' Nishant's concern was churning my stomach.

'Let's just write them lyrics, yeah?'

If you could see we could be together
You would see I be asking you whether
The night that shines is like a bright measure
Of the darkness of your beauty forever
I could love you but I have loved others
I would never choose you over my brothers
But why why why can't we love?
Why why why can't we fly to heaven above?
Love is a wonderful thing
Brings more pain but it brings
Joy and ecstasy
I hope you love me

'That's beautiful,' said Anand. 'She's gonna love it man, thank you. You're a true brother.'

'Ha!' I laughed, just that extra piquant slice of knowing on my tastebuds. 'Make sure she don't find out you got help.'

'Listen man, I'm sure she's got friends we can introduce you to. You know for some of that . . . summit-summit.'

'All good man. For now, the time is Coconut Unlimited. Later's the time for all the girlies to fall at my feet, ya get me?'

*   *   *

Anand called me up, after dinner. I was re-reading a Nas interview and listening to the album, trying to muster some enthusiasm to study.

'Meena *freaked* when I read her my poem! She said it's the most beautiful thing she's ever heard.'

'For real?'

'You cupid man.'

'Safe bro.' I was pulling at some wallpaper behind the phone table. The more I tore off, the bigger the patch of white wall became.

'Can she come to the next practice?'

'What?' I wanted to sack him there and then. 'We haven't done a practice yet cos you've been off tonguing her too much to care.'

'OK . . . can she come to the second practice then?'

*   *   *

Ahmed and I were walking between classes, silent. I turned to him.

'Listen, Ahmed. Do you like Pentil?'

'What do you mean?'

'Well, before you guys showed up, he used to call Anand, Nishant and me the 'Paki Posse', and whisper 'budbudbudbud' whenever we walked past. Now you guys are around, he doesn't do that anymore. I'm just, like, what's going on with him?'

'Pentil's not a racist, man. He just doesn't like you. He thinks you're a bit soulless and try-hard.'

'Man, that's just how we talk round the way.'

'Listen, Amit, you're alright. You're a sweet guy. We're all going to a party this weekend. Why don't you come and show Pentil you're a nice guy? He just needs to spend some time with you. Come with us.'

'Yeah, alright,' I replied, having every intention of making up an excuse at the last minute.

*   *   *

Amazingly, Anand turned up for practice. Annoyingly, he'd brought a girl with him.

'Amit, this is Meena. Meena, this is Amit. You've met Nishant already . . . '

'Anand tells me you're in his band . . . ?' she said, smiling.

'*His* band?'

'So, are you guys gonna, like, rap and stuff now?'

'Anand, I don't think she should be here – you know, keep some suspense while we're still working stuff out.'

'Oh it'll be like I'm not here. I wanna hear my boy in action.'

This was the first time we'd tried me rapping my own lyrics, and I'd been working on some new ones. This time it was going to work because I'd come up with a new tactic. I grabbed a pen, ready for the beat to drop, held it to my lips like a microphone, gripping it between my knuckles, my index finger and little finger, then faced the French windows leading to the rose bush-ambushed garden, like I was facing a crowd, but actually so I wasn't facing them, my peers, my band. I was ready.

A Dre instrumental dropped, all squelchy synths and fried laconic plinking plonking pianos over a simple but languid beat. It was summer in California. I got ready, closed my eyes, felt the instrumental surge through me. I could see my fans, a crowd divided in two; women waving jiggling bodyparts in my general direction to the left of me, rowdy bowdy boyz anteing up on my right. I was ready, they were ready, Anand was ready and Dangerous had dropped the beat.

> *Dangerous drops the beat, I drop heat*
> *Like a pile of burning spaghetti on your white sheets*
> *You Ku Klux Klan motherfucker*
> *I get you down like a dead trucker*
> *You're in luck, chump, I saw her rump, it's mine first*
> *I got the taste, I got the thirst, I'm about to . . .*
> *I wish that we could be together forever*
> *If we could then you would be my treasure . . .*

Anand burst in with his love poem lyrics. I turned round to find Nishant spinning and twirling as best as he could on carpet, and Anand croon-rapping the lyrics I'd written for him out of time with the beat, holding Meena's chin and staring at her seductively. She clapped in rapture. I hit the 'stop' button.

'We're not doing that song yet. We're doing "We Got The Gunz We Got The Planz", until you jumped in, you prick.'

'Yeah, sorry, I was just looking at Meena and I couldn't contain myself. I needed to come out.' Nishant giggled at the innuendo. I stared at Meena. She was messing up our flow. She had to go.

'You have to go.'

'Amit, don't be rude, she's not causing any harm.'

'She's distracting you – that's enough for me.'

'Listen, if I go, Anand comes with me, right?'

'OK fine, stay, but can we carry on with "We Got The Gunz We Got The Planz" like we said we would please? Thank you.'

I collected myself. Anand put his foot up on the sofa between Meena's restless legs, crouching down to wink at her. Yeah, she was kinda buff. But still, SO brown.

The music started up again.

> *Dangerous drops the beat, I drop heat*
> *Like a pile of burning spaghetti on your white sheets*
> *You Ku Klux Klan motherfucker*

YEEEAAAH COCO-Nu-HUUUTTT

Anand was steaming around the room, moshing invisible bodies out of the way, streaming through the dance. I tried to carry on.

> *I get you down like a dead trucker*
> *You're in luck, chump, I saw her rump, it's mine first*
> *I got the taste, I got the thirst, I'm about to burst*
> *You're in luck, chump, I saw her rump, it's mine first*
> *I got the taste, I got the thirst, I'm about to burst*
> *You're the worst, you wear white shirts*
> *When I hear the cops coming, I splurt . . .*

YEEEAAAH COCO-Nu-HUUUTTT

Anand was all over the place, trying to mount the small pool table, a cacophony of energy commanding the eyes of the room, a rambunctuous centrafugal force of attention-seeking. Nishant was oblivious, in the middle of attempting a carpeted moonwalk. Anand was grinding and flaying his hips like a Chippendale who'd been doused in hot oil. Because of his antics, no one could see that I was nearly rapping in time.

I stopped. Nishant stopped. Meena burst out laughing. Anand, with his eyes closed, took a few more seconds to cotton on. Nishant faded the music down and we both stared at the giggling girl and her male stripper. Anand looked at us.

'Is practice nearly done yet? I've got an empty house for like, fifty more minutes . . . '

'Oh my God, baby, we need to go.'

'Believe. Listen, Amit, Dangerous, sounding good but we'll pick this up tomorrow. I'll finish those love lyrics tonight, I think I'm gonna be inspired . . . ' He winked at Meena. She got up, linked his arm, and they left.

Nishant took the record off the deck and carefully placed it in its cover, putting it on a shelf of records and CDs proudly labelled 'NISHANT' in graffiti-style lettering.

'I guess that's it for today then . . . '

'I guess so,' I replied.

What was I going to do now? The only option was returning home to Mum and the regime of study-study-buddy-buddy.

We looked at each other with a look that said, 'It's just not the same without Anand is it?'

I put my shoes on, grabbed my coat and Walkman and headed home, listening intently to the instrumentals, trying to figure out the science of drum-beats and how rappers flowed to the beat, a mystery to me, still, that fundamental tool of my self-professed trade.

*   *   *

Home was alive when I jived in through the front door.

Mum's friend Vijay was visiting, this time with her super sexy daughter Ekta. Well, sexy for an Asian girl. She was small with actual green eyes – not the fake lame contact lenses that other girls wore. She also had a bit of a Jamaican bumper, curving outwards like a half-tyre, or a car bumper. She wore a denim jacket and a T-shirt with a ninja on it, and her sandals showed off her toes; tiny little chipolatas dressed in thick lacquered burgundy varnish.

I asked if she wanted to leave the boring adults to their boring gossip and she reluctantly followed me up to my room, egged on by both our mums, spying a caste-perfect match. I didn't know her that well, having met her only a few times and being too shy to really talk to her.

She looked a little put out as I gestured to my desk chair for her to sit, while I lounged empirically on the bed, legs akimbo, socks vaporising into the atmosphere. She shifted the pile of clothes, shuffling them to the floor with the least amount of skin-contact possible. I saw some of my white boxers, stained with the cream haze of late-night BBC2 art porn, land on top of the pile. I jumped up and grabbed the pile, offering to get them out of the way, falling back on the bed as nonchalantly as letting a guest sit on my cum-stained pants would allow. I flipped on the tape recorder and Nas came on.

'Oh, you like hip-hop . . . ' she shrugged, slightly disappointed.

'Yeah, why? Don't you?'

'Not really. Just, you know, Bollywood and stuff.'

'Oh right, *typical Asian*,' I said in my budbudbud voice.

'Anyway . . . how are you Amit?'

'Oh, you know, straight chillin' . . . you know me.'

'Not really.'

'Got a boyfriend?'

'That's a bit of a personal question, Amit.'

'Sorry, well, just checking innit.'

'Why? You interested?'

'I ain't got time to be interested, ya get me?' I was building up to telling her about my band. She sighed. Audible laughter from downstairs shifted her attention to our mums, having a better time than us. 'You know,' I continued, 'what with my band and everything . . . '

I hadn't wanted to drop the line about being in a band too early. I needed to build up an air of nonchalance before igniting her loins with the declaration that yes, I was in a band – and yes, I was *pretty cool*.

'Oh right, do you gig much?' she asked, clearly not interested.

'Nah. Still writing, still getting ready to unleash.'

'Wow . . . '

'It's gonna be big.'

She turned to look at me. 'You do realise how slim a chance you have of making it don't you? You do realise music is impossible to get into? You do realise you're fourteen, you live in Harrow and you're Asian? You do realise all these things? Plus, who listens to hip-hop?' She picked at her nails, refusing to make eye contact with me.

I stared at her. I could get angry, I thought, but then it ruined any chance of keeping Ekta onside. She was different to the rest. She talked different. She was more erudite, eloquent, despite all the Bollywood rubbish she listened to. I could live with that. I just needed to amuse her, to make her realise I was gonna be someone, someone she could definitely fancy. I just needed proof of some sort somewhere that at least one girl, a minimum of one girl out there in the universe, could find me even remotely attractive. I told everyone I wasn't using the band to get girls, but the truth of it was the band *was* to get girls' attention – but the attention of girls beyond the slim remit of Harrow, worldy (and preferably white) girls, who liked hip-hop. A tall order, but they had to exist, surely.

'Mind if I open a window?' she asked, breaking me out of my dream state. I wondered what could possibly happen now. I mean, I could help her open the window, grab her hand and pull her towards the bed. I could ask her to join me on the bed. I could start crying about Ash and Pentil and everything, to show her my vulnerable side and hope she'd comfort me. Or, I could ask her about her dead dad till she cried, then comfort *her*. God, the opportunities were endless. I mean, I really could get my leg over here, I thought. All I needed to do was pick an avenue, stick with it and go full throttle.

'So, Ekta, how's things?'

'God Amit, I was having a better conversation downstairs listening to your mum talk about her menopause. Come on, you can do better. Try again.'

'Whatever girl, you're the one with nothing to say.'

'Ask me what the last film I saw was; ask me what I'm doing in biology; ask me what shoes I'm wearing. God . . . '

More talk. Great.

'OK, what are you doing in biology?'

'The digestive system. You?'

'Erm . . . sexual reproduction?' I don't know why I phrased it as a question but in my brain it sounded so hot, till I heard the syllables coming out my mouth and added the question mark to indicate my confusion.

'Really? Now we're getting somewhere. Right, and what bit are you doing?'

'The inside of the penis.'

'Look, Amit. You're lovely but call me when you know how to talk to a girl, OK?'

'I know myself. What are you talking about girl?'

She stood up, snarled at the pile of clothes and walked out. God, Finchley girls were so hot.

I stared at where she sat and bounded over, putting my hand in the warmth of her seat, imagining the bum that had been parked there. My hand on her bum-patch seat-heat was the closest I'd ever been to kissing a girl.

I reached for the dried-cum boxers.

*   *   *

Saturday afternoon, the day of the party with Jasel and Ahmed, and my stomach was fluctuating. It was like waves of electricity in an evil scientist's laboratory. Mum had been on at me all day about some coursework I'd accidentally mentioned that needed doing. Dad had been his usual stoic self, but because it was the weekend his work/staring into space was augmented by daytime cans of lukewarm Foster's, his weekend vice. My sister had been on the phone all day and I'd wanted to call Anand to find out if he was about or with Yoko Meena. Nishant was away in the countryside with his parents, rambling and strawberry-picking. I'd been inside, anxiety-ating about this party and how it could all go down.

Whose party were we going to? Would I be expected to drink or smoke drugs? Would I be too pissed to get home? Where was the party? Was it far? Could I walk home? Would I need a taxi? What time was the last bus? Could you get a bus to the party from Harrow? Where? Who was going? Was Pentil going? What should I wear? Hip-hop or preppie? Would there be girls there? Would I be able to talk to them? Would they all have boyfriends? Would they all be white at the party? What was going to be my excuse for not drinking beer? What if I liked beer too much? What if people were smoking and the smoke stayed in my hair and I came home stinking of cigarettes? Would Mum think it was weird if I had a shower at, like, 1 a.m. to get the smell out? Would I be home by 1 a.m.?

Round and round my head these thoughts went, endlessly pounding and pumping and remonstrating and picketing like disgruntled socialists.

Deep down I knew I wasn't going.

*   *   *

BRRRING–BRRRING–BRRRING

I was startled out of bed, after midnight. I ran to the phone and grabbed it.

'Hello?' I whispered.

'Yo, Amit, where you at?' I could hear laughter and music in the background – groany guitar shit.

'Jasel?'

'Where you at? You on your way?'

'Ahh man, I couldn't make it . . . I . . . '

'Tell him he's a paki plum!' I heard Pentil squeal in the background, hilarity erupting around him.

'It's a shame you didn't come,' said Jasel. 'We had a girl lined up for you, ready to give you your first kiss.'

My mouth sapped dry. 'Right.'

'She wants to talk to you. Talk to her.'

'Oh, nah man . . . I can't, I'm not . . . '

'Hello?' The voice was husky, stifling giggles, wobbly and most definitely female.

I breathed heavily.

'Is that Amit?'

'Yeah, safe.'

In the background, 'Has he started talking all wigga-ry now?'

'Yeah . . . I can't, I can't . . . ' she said, laughing. 'It's too jokes.'

'Who's this anyway?' I said, ignoring the voices.

'It's Nat.'

'Alright Nat.'

'Yeah, listen, Jasel told me how sexy you are and Pentil said you're well good at sports and stuff. And I love Indian men, they're so sexy and dark and beautiful and chocolatey like milk chocolate. So when we going out?'

'What? I don't know you.'

'Listen, I could just meet you and we could, you know, snog. How old are you? And you've never been snogged? Poor baby . . . ' Her voice faltered, stifling the giggles.

'IS AHMED THERE?!'

'Don't you wanna talk to me baby?'

'Listen, let man talk to Jasel.'

Jasel came back on the phone. 'Sexy huh?'

'Jasel you're such a prick.' I slammed the phone down.

BRRRING–BRRRING–BRRRING

'It's for me,' I hissed, and picked it up.

'I'm gonna make your life a living hell.' CLICK-BRRRRRR RRRR . . .

'Jasel?'

* * *

Monday morning at school and I had heartburn, the hulking fear that my life was going to be made a living hell. What was Jasel going to do to me? Would Ahmed be complicit in this whole thing? He'd been eerily silent on Saturday night. I hadn't dared phone either of them the next day and the ringing-phone-silence-hang-up that permeated Sunday as I hid indoors was enough to scare me. Was he to make good on his threat, or was he going to just laugh it all off as a big nothing?

I walked up the corridor in a daze as Anand and Nishant strode akimbo, discussing weekends. I hadn't told them what had happened yet. They were obliviously and deliriously regaling me with tales of late night boobie sightings on television while trying to watch *Boyz n the Hood* on rented VHS.

It came to my turn to share and I timed it with the door to my classroom. I shrugged a 'laters' at them and pushed the door open, wandering into one of the crickball games' many semi-finals. Everyone looked up at me and returned to their game.

Sigh-relief, news of my pussy-ness hadn't spread yet. There was an acidic churn in my stomach, a wilting burn of impending doom solidified into undigestable dread cakes. No Jasel. No Ahmed. No Pentil. The clock edged closer to their imminent arrival before BS. I tinkered with some homework I'd half-concentrated on with panic and anxiety over the weekend and waited. Dread dread dread in my head head head.

PUSH-KICK-OPEN-SWING . . .

Jasel, Ahmed and Pentil all walked in, smiling. I hadn't even considered being bolshy and pissed off with them. I was mired in the worry of their power and status and what they could do to make me look like an even bigger loser than usual. Something that not even Coconut Unlimited could save me from. They all smiled at me enigmatically, Mona Lisa mystery. Would they be taking the piss out of me? Usually Ahmed sat next to me, with Jasel by himself at the desk in front. Not today. They were headed for the central Pentil hub concentrated in the middle of the room, the middle row of desks being filled with his cronies and now two new additions. They sat down and laughed about something.

'Hey Amit!'

'Hey Jasel. You OK?'

'Fantastic. You?'

'Yeah, I'm fine.'

'You mean you're not *safe blud*?' They all laughed. 'Are you ready for life to become hell?'

'What?' I said, turning. 'I don't understand . . . '

'You embarrassed me in front of my friends, my real life friends, and there will be consequences.'

'Whatever Jasel. What's the point?'

'The point is, my dear Amit, you're a gormless prick who thinks he's black. That's worse than acting like a gora.'

PUSH-SHOVE-OPEN-SWING . . .

BS entered as I shot a final glance at the new additions to my torment. Pentil was uninterested, flicking through the *Sun*, and Ahmed was looking straight ahead, stoney-faced.

Jasel blew me a kiss.

*   *   *

Despite my efforts to disappear into my studies, I had nowhere to hide. My endeavours, like rinsing Latin tests or actually remembering to do my Maths homework, were undermined by Jasel trying to wet-kiss me behind the ear at every opportunity. His threat was largely silent. He'd pass me notes with rap suggestions, ones that suggested I was 'gay'. He'd wink at me whenever our eyes met. Meanwhile Pentil had turned to calling me 'Gorma Korma'. Ahmed was mute. I didn't even have Coconut Unlimited to distract me because Anand was spending more time with Meena and, without him, Nishant's motivation waned.

The change came halfway through the second week of my torture when Jasel's wet-kiss lunges became more sluggish, and

Pentil's name-calling suddenly stopped. Ahmed remained mute, but red-eyed. They were all red-eyed.

The other development was more alarming. Whenever I now walked through Harrow and saw Ash, he'd make every effort to come over and daps me on the fist, like we were buddies. I didn't need the association. Troubling though it was, it did, however, fill me with a little bravado in the face of the name-calling, bodily violations and insulting notes.

It was all confusing. I dealt with it all in silence, my head filled with rap lyrics, my crew disappeared into their own lives. I was locked in a fortress of solitude.

It was the worst of times, it was the worst of times.

*   *   *

Oh the indignity of it all. A Saturday night and Mum and Dad had finally convinced me to come with them to a family event. This time it was a Brahmin mixer at Edgware Country Club, a classier affair than usual Harrow shenanigans. I felt guilty for always avoiding the events despite Mum telling me I needed to spend more time with my own people and not those 'bevakoofs'.

The country club had once been a source of great white golfing hopes, but its proximity to the Gujarati hub of North West London and its reasonable room-hire prices meant it had become a function hall for Indians to celebrate weddings, birthdays, religious conversions and dinner and dances; my worst nightmare, where lukewarm chicken curry was served to drunk middle-aged moustache-ridden Indians and their grumpy children, who'd spend the evenings elaborately trying to sneak off for snogging, cigarettes and alcohol, the behaviour of the normal teenager but so taboo, so naughty, that it felt about forty per cent more serious than normal.

I was there, my sister was there, Ravi was there, Ravi's sister was there and . . . that was it. No Anand, no Nishant, no crew. Only Bollywood and bhangra and my mum and dad grinning wildly as they presented themselves to the community. Nish disappeared into her giggling birdcage of suffocation and slinky Gujarati girlies, all young and younger and dumb and dumber, while Ravi was off trying to convince Sudha to come and dance with him and consider being a treasurer for the Young Gujaratis.

I was left with Shalini, Ravi's sister. We were talking about not much, mostly television, the go-to subject for those with nothing in common. Her friend Natasha sat mute next to her, in a sari with a leather jacket draped over her shoulders like a country club accessory. She peered out into the darkened dancefloor watching the middle-aged demonstrate to each other that they single-handedly hadn't lost the party spirit. They danced with their wives, with their eyes shifting to their extreme rights and lefts watching anyone who appeared to be having a better time than them. Their dancing enthusiasm was reserved for the more modern sounding Bollywood songs, not the classics they remembered only fondly.

'This is so lame,' Shalini mumbled.

'So boring, I know,' said Natasha, a young-looking girl with fuzzy black hair, chipped black nails and innocent child eyes.

'Innit,' I added absently.

'Let's bounce,' Shalini said, standing up. 'We'll get Ajit to buy us vodka cokes.'

'It's Amit actually . . . '

I tutted. Boozehounds and try-hards everywhere. I knew I should have stayed at home and practised rapping on Dad's decent hi-fi. The problem was, if I'd stayed at home, they would've told me to look after Nish and she would've hogged the telly. I wouldn't have been able to pump the hi-fi up to 20dB and scream out my rap lyrics like a proper gangsta. Instead I was surrounded by Bale-Bale, the guttural man-cry of bhangra music, a shout you had to yelp from your primordial centre to show everyone you were having a good time and enjoying the good music.

We started to walk away and Natasha disappeared into the crowd. Shalini held a hand up to my chest, stopping me.

'You know, Natasha will snog you if you ask.'

'What?'

'She's desperate for a snog and said you'd do. Everyone else is busy pretending to have an awesome time. She wanted to snog Ravi but he's gone off with that Sudha bitch.'

'She'll snog me?'

'Yeah, just ask her.'

'What the . . . what?'

She shrugged, turned round like she was a sexy genie and walked off sashaying her pendulum bottom from side to side.

A snog. Oh.

The familiar cramp in my stomach, the Jasel cramp, returned, along with a second skin of sweat. I leaned forward, easing the cramp that was now travelling up my erect dick and down to my perineum. That space between my balls and bum was a thick knot of anxiety and arousal, the biggest mixed message my body could bother to bestow on me. Balls.

I followed the girls, subtly loosening my belt buckle by one notch. They were waiting for me in the derelict lobby of the country club. Everyone was inside shouting 'hooba hooba hooba' to a 70s Bollywood song currently reinvigorated by a hard house techno remix. The toilets were eerily quiet.

'How best to play this, Amit?' I thought to myself. 'Stay cool, remember you *are* cool. You're in a band for God's sake . . . '

'I'm in a band,' I said to no one in particular.

'Samit, wanna go for a walk?' Natasha bit her lip and smiled at me. How old was she? Like, thirteen or something?

'Amit,' Shalini corrected her.

'Amit?'

'Yeah,' I added, not looking at her.

'Wanna go for a walk?'

'OK . . . ' I swaggered towards the door, stopped and turned round, offering my hand and saying smoothly, 'You coming baby?'

103

Except she was right behind me and my romantic gesture became a punch in the tit, or lack thereof. We smiled awkwardly. I went into auto-pilot. No time to panic/celebrate about my first ever snog, bitches. Yes! Screw you Jasel! Up yours Pentil! Pity you Ahmed! Kiss my arse, Anand . . . I'll get my own bitch now and I won't turn up to band practice now neither.

'So what-what-wh-what school do you go to?' I asked, my mouth suddenly dry. I needed to preserve mouth moisture for the saliva spot, so my plan was to ask loads of questions.

'Oh, I don't live in London. Rochdale. Why? You wanna come visit?'

'How old are you?'

'Old enough to not be doing this for the first time, darling. This your first?'

'Nah, girl, course not.'

'Look, I'm doing this cos you're the only one around. I really needed a snog. I'm not no teacher or nothin'.'

'Whatever girl.' I held on to any sense of bravado with the most brittle of fingernails. 'How old are you?'

'Fourteen.'

'Yeah, safe . . . '

The car park was dimly lit and the night wasn't particularly pleasant. I rued not grabbing my coat. She had her sari, a leather jacket and a bigger person's puffa jacket. I was in my best 'smart' shirt and trousers, and I was cold.

We crept to the end of the car park where the golf course started and the floodlights alleviated. We were silent. I was mentally working out how low to stoop to reach her lips and whether this would mean less contact with her body, which was both warm and boobed; despite the lack of boobs per se, she still had boobs. We stopped. She walked in front of me and looked up, waiting for the expert to lean down and tear her lips apart with fiery kisses. I quickly gargled the last of the saliva in my mouth for moisture and leaned in, unsure. She put her hand on the back of my head and thrust me forward, banging our teeth together and shivering us both. Her mouth felt like tonguing wet jelly; not pleasant. Her tongue was hovering just inside my mouth, while my overly enthusiastic juggernaut tongue erupted like an alien into hers. She pulled away.

'Not so rough.'

'Man's a man,' I whispered half-heartedly.

'Just slow down.'

My stomach was fizzing. 'Can I put my hand on your bum?' I asked, my dick electric with nerves and nerve-endings.

'If you want to.' She shrugged a little.

I placed my hands on her bum and made my move. It still felt slightly odd, the sensations of kissing; not quite there yet, all teeth and tongue monoliths fighting for attention. I leaned in further, shivering, and she opened her coat up and I placed my hands on her back, warm. I moved back down to her bony teenage bum and smiled. I was true gangsta. I squeezed. She pulled away.

'My brother might see us.'

'Oh, right.'

'We should go back inside. He's probably looking for me.'

'Who's your brother?'

'Jay.'

'Oh . . . '

'Do you know him?'

'Not being funny but there's a lot of people in that room called Jay.'

'Well we should get back, in case he's looking for me.'

I turned and in the dark tried to grab her hand, but it wasn't where it should've been. She'd crossed her arms and walked away, in front of me by a few steps.

What just happened? I got snogged – that's what . . .

Shalini was waiting for us as we reentered the country club. Wow, I thought, an Indian vixen. Ice cold. She managed to convince me to snog her in, like, two minutes. Maybe they ain't all bad.

'Better?' she asked Natasha.

'I guess.' She turned and smiled at me sweetly.

'So should I call you?' I asked.

'Only if you're planning to come to Rochdale . . . '

'Is that near London?'

She laughed and wandered off. Shalini turned to me.

'So?'

'So what?'

'Have a nice time?'

'You know, Indian girls are alright . . . '

'You're such a coconut.'

'I'm just saying . . . '

The end-of-the-night bhangra music hit its crescendo, and I headed back to my table to wait for my sister and parents to stop embarrassing me with their bud-bud ways. Natasha had disappeared into the night. It was almost like it never happened, and it might as well not have happened, given the way I was going to spin this story on Monday morning.

Now I was a man.

Next: Gigging opportunities

CHAPTER FIVE

Live at the Barbeque

'This is every month?'
  'Yeah.'
  'And it's open mic?'
  'Yeah.'
  'So anyone can turn up?'
  'Yeah.'
  'And do whatever they want?'
  'Yeah.'
  'In the Fat Controller?'
  'Yeah. Upstairs.'
  'So we could just turn up, sign up and rock the house?'
  'Yeah.'
  'And Eddy reckons we can rock the hip-hop there?'
  'Yeah. He reckons we need to do it, like a training ground.'
  'How you mean?'
  'Like, we won't know what works and what doesn't work till we do it in front of strangers.'
  'Nishant, I think we know what works and what doesn't work already. We'll do it, though. Time to spread the fan base a bit wider, ya get me?'
  'You're very quiet Anand . . . '
  Nishant turned to MC AP. He'd been sitting at the table with his arms crossed, staring into space. The arcade was fizzy with excitement today. Everyone was out. Ash was holding court. Even Pentil, Jasel and Ahmed were around, sending weird burns through my stomach. They couldn't know they'd shook me, though, and with my boys by my side I could hold ground

propped up by their bluster. In any case, I knew Ash had my back. He'd come up to me the week after Pentil had started showing up for weed and taken me to one side.

'Listen, you need to man up. When this band comes round, I better be so proud I want to take my T-shirt off and throw it at you. Till then you need to man up.'

'What?'

'You see, this white man you've introduced me to, he's gonna be coming round the way for weed. Now he's not a fan of yours. I told him you're fam. We're Guji, Brahmin, we stick together. I got no time for him or his Muslim mosquito friend or his coconut blud, seen? You're my brother. They're my transactions. So you're safe, I got your back. But in school, man got to man up or get manned.'

'Yeah, safe.'

'Good, now run along and let me run my bidness.'

Knowing volatile Ash was on my side gave me safety in his numbers of pectorals. Keeping him on side meant being polite, always saying hello then keeping visible but out of speaking distance. And if he wanted to know what I was up to, I just said band stuff, which he respected. We were a family in Harrow. I may have been the embarrassed kid desperate to escape his strange uncle, but he was still family and it was comforting to know we stuck together. Plus he was actually real-life family with Anand. Anand's first cousin's brother-in-law married Ash's brother's wife's niece, meaning they called each other's parents 'Auntie' and 'Uncle', 'Mami' and 'Mama'.

Nishant prodded Anand, who was still quiet.

'Yeah, I'm OK. Things got a little weird with Meena.'

'How so?'

'She's just, like, she always wants to spend time with me and, like, talk to me on the phone and I realised something the other day when we'd been sitting in silence on the phone for, like, seven minutes, watching telly holding the phone . . . we don't have much to talk about.'

'What? You're the hypeman in a badboy hip-hop band. You got loads to talk about.' I couldn't believe the only one with a girlfriend wasn't using his band credentials to get some.

'Except we ain't done no tunes.'

'Whose fault is that?'

'All I'm saying is, it's hard to find stuff to talk about if all we do is talk and spend time together and I got no time to live a life I can talk to her about. It's perplexing.'

'Good word,' Nishant chirped. 'Perplexing. Per-plexing. You should get that in one of the rappings.'

'Listen man, we just need to put in some time, rehearse for this gig, tear the roof off, standardly, and then she'll be all over you.'

'She's all over me now. I just, you know, want to do something else. It's boring now. She kisses nine times out of ten the exact same way – tongue moving in and out slowly like a Super Mario retractable platform made of soft lips. And she wants to do it for hours.'

'So anyway,' I interrupted, sick. 'Let's plan this gig.'

'I can put together a dance move for it!'

'Nishant, man, you're the DJ. You'll be scratching and stuff.'

'Yeah . . . I should learn how to do that.'

'How many songs can we do for the open mic?' I said, refocusing us quickly, like a leader.

'Two I think,' said Nishant.

'Cool, so we do "We Got the Planz We Got the Gunz" and what else?'

'Can I do "Love is a Wonderful Thing"?' said Anand.

'What's that? That's not a Coconut joint . . . '

'It's the joint you wrote for me to write for Meena. She'd love it.'

'Nah man, you do your own open mic. This is band styles. We're all in this together. I think we'll do "Girls Get Tackled".'

'But that ain't finished yet. The lyrics . . . ' Anand was trying his luck, pushing for 'Love is a Wonderful Thing'.

'They is. I finished 'em last night.'

And she was, like, baby I like it raw
I said I'd rather cook it just to be sure
And she was, like, baby I wanna suck it all
And I was, like, baby, you make me go stand tall
And she was, like, baby, sorry, I'm smelling like mackerel
Don't worry baby baby, girls get tackled . . .

I opened my eyes. Nishant stood up and applauded enthusiastically. Anand sat there and nodded his head in agreement.

'Yes, bro. It's there. We're doing that.' We did that side-high-five where we slap then click each other's fingers.

'Amit,' Nishant said, his hands clasped together. 'How do you do it? How do your words make so much sense when the world is a mess of crazy relationships and war and just . . . life. It's amazing.'

'Safe bro.'

I felt a peripheral burn in my stomach and looked over to Ash. Pentil and Jasel had entered the arcade and were heading towards him. Jasel blew a kiss at me, which I ignored as I imagined it slobbering over my cheek. I turned to my boys.

'Right, we need a tight band schedule. We're gonna blow the roof off the Fat Controller.'

*   *   *

'Yo Amit, can I borrow you for a sec?'

I looked over my shoulder and saw Mark Herman, a hirsute teenager with an answer for everything, standing nervously next to me, his eyes filmed with whisps of red underneath a milky glaze of water. It was breaktime. I'd just finished putting my tray of half-eaten food on the collection table and was feeling guilty about succumbing to infidel beef, but the chilli con carne was offensively tasty. Anand was on lunchtime detention for drawing a nude of Meena for his art homework and Nishant was behind stage-left in the school hall learning martial arts from Jason Aye, a year below student with an infinite knowledge of martial arts and twenty per cent vision through his thick glasses. I was alone and avoiding Jasel and Pentil till the bell rang.

'What's up, Herman?'

He stifled a giggle. 'So, Amit, listen . . . can you sort me out with some stuff?'

'What kinda stuff?'

'Err . . . well . . . '

'Drugs? Do you think just cos I'm brown I'm a drug dealer? You're Jewish, Herman. You should understand about being oppressed, you racist.'

'No, you dickhead. Some hip-hop tapes. I really like it and thought you'd be the guy with the tapes. Can you tape me some stuff?'

'Really?'

'Yeah.'

'You're not taking the mick?'

'Nah, man. Listen, I just like it, you know. I get it now.' Herman said, pumping a fist in the air. He giggled. 'Fuck the police. Ha!'

'Yeah, well. I can do you a mixtape. What kinda bam?'

'Whatever you think's good man. Educate me.'

*　　*　　*

We walked out of Jammin with Edwards and headed back towards St George's, feeling the warmth from the new vinyl Nishant had in his bag.

'Herman's into hip-hop now?' Anand was incredulous.

'Maybe he just likes it, guys.' Nishant shrugged. 'Like, you know, *I* just like it.'

I wasn't sure it was that easy. He used to call hip-hop 'shit-hop', like he was a stand-up comedian.

'Maybe all that weed's making him like repetitive drums and low bass. My dad told me that's why reggae sounds good when you're stoned. Cos it's like all you hear are the low noises and the high noises and the repetitive beat stops you from falling over.'

Anand and I turned to look at Nishant.

'He used to smoke weed as a teenager,' he offered, by way of explanation.

'Is Herman a stoner now?'

'Yeah of course man. They all walk down to the lake before and after school and sometimes at lunchtime, and smoke. That's why you don't see Pentil and Jasel at lunch anymore.'

I couldn't believe it. Surely this was because of my connecting him with Ash. I'd inadvertently neutralised him.

'Yeah. Pentil's been selling loads of weed to everyone.'

'How do you know all of this stuff man?' I demanded.

'Well, Jason and I decided for kung-fu club we'd do some water training, like fighting in water, just to build up our upper-body strength and I saw them all down there, but luckily Jason knew how to move stealthily like a ninja so we ninja-stealth-walked over to the bushes, near where they all hide, and we listened in on the conversations and it was definitely Pentil selling it all to Herman and Jamie Woodcliffe and Jasel and Richard Miles and Darren Durrant and Michael Barry and Paul Whatmuff.'

'Whatmuff? That dweeb?' Anand couldn't believe the only kid shorter than him in the year was such a bad boy.

'I heard he has teenage arthritis.'

'So you reckon that all these stoners are gonna start liking hip-hop now?' Anand said.

'Why wouldn't they? I mean, like, Dr Dre had that album about smoking and Cypress Hill do songs about smoking . . . '

I was indignant. I mean, one minute they're all listening to whiny guitar rubbish and now, cos they smoked some weed, they liked hip-hop. And not even the good stuff about revolution and politics and intelligence. Just crap about smoking weed. It was a mockery.

'Or . . . ' Anand piped up, 'it's a good opportunity.'

We both turned to him as we turned the corner.

'We make mixtapes. We start with, like, a Coconut Unlimited intro, like, "Wassup wassup this is Coconut Unlimited, we got the gunz, we got the planz and you're listening to this mixtape we made for you. Hope you like it. PEACE BITCHES." And then we do a mixtape that starts with some stoner hip-hop stuff like Dre and Snoop then we get into some of the heavy stuff like Public Enemy . . . '

'And Lords of the Underground.'

'Yes, Nishant, and Lords of the Underground, then we end with one of our own tunes.'

'We could be rich,' I said, realising the potential. 'And, it's good promo for the open mic.'

We were nearly home. I loved walking from school with Anand and Nishant. It felt so much nicer than being picked up by Mum and having the day's study points picked apart, usually ending in her threatening to send me to Gayton High School, a comprehensive in the middle of Harrow town centre housing mostly Gujaratis.

'We should call the mixtape "Volume 15",' I said, 'so people think there's fourteen other mixtapes and we've been doing it for time and they're bandwagon jumpers.'

'Yeah, but do we have to record fifteen different mixtapes? I'm not sure we have enough records . . . ' Why did Nishant always ask such dumb-ass questions?

'No, we don't actually record fourteen more mixtapes. We create mystique. People'll be, like, damn where do I get volumes one-to-fourteen and we're, like, sorry dude, out of print, out of stock, done dusted, look out for volume sixteen . . . '

'BIG!' Anand got excited. 'Mystique' was a word that always pricked up his tiny ears.

'We just need to get a recording of "We Got the Gunz We Got the Planz", and I got a mic. It's in my bag.'

I'd noticed a microphone socket on the front of Nishant's dad's stereo, and I knew from childhood experience that all you needed was some headphones and, if you talked into the right ear, it'd pick up as a recording.

We were going to make our first tune and it was going to sound amazing. 'We Got the Gunz We Got the Planz' would be done over a Nas instrumental we'd procured, and I was excited. I'd nearly sorted out my flow problems and my issues with rapping in time. All Anand had to do was shout 'Coconut Unlimited' repeatedly in the background and if Nishant wanted to stand to one side and dance he was welcome to. I had an actual microphone device and a reason to record now. I had the *planz*. Not only that but everyone in the school was going to hear *my* song and they'd think I was *pretty cool* now. Gone would be the 'Black Beauty' and 'Gorma Korma' and 'Chuckles' nicknames. Gone would be the jokes about my side-parting quiff. Gone. All gone. Eff you school. I'm your new leader while Pentil's off getting stoned and listening to my choons. I run the corridors.

'Do you need a rehearsal?'

'Nah, we've been going through this song for a minute now. I'm ready. Run it . . . wait, no, press 'record', then drop the needle, then I'm coming in. Yeah?' I mentally prepared myself.

'Yeah.'

'Nandy Pandy, you ready?'

'YEEEEEEEEEEAAAAAAAAAAAHHHHHHHHHH.' Anand was jumping up and down, darting back, back and forth and forth.

'Cool. Shut the door. Nishant, where's your mum?'

'She and Tejal are at Botany Club.'

'Right, we ready?' I felt the mood in the air, the electrons buzzing in my ears and mouth.

Nishant leaned over me. I was holding my foam earphones, my mouth pressed up near the speaker ready to unleash. He pressed record. There was the slightest pregnant pause and he placed the needle delicately on the vinyl. Warmness, fuzziness, crackle and fiz . . .

BOOM BAP BOOM BOOM BAP
BOOM BAP BOOM BOOM BAP
BOOM BAP BOOM BOOM BAP

BOOM BAP BOOM BOOM BAP
BOOM BAP BOOM BOOM BAP
BOOM BAP BOOM BOOM BAP
BOOM BAP BOOM BOOM BAP
BOOM BAP BOOM BOOM BAP

Nishant pressed 'stop' on the vinyl.

'You ready dude?'

'Yeah yeah yeah . . . sorry, just preparing myself.' I turned to Anand. 'I'm nervous.'

'Don't be a pussy, man. Think of all the pussy.' He grinned and thrusted his hips.

Nishant put his hand on my shoulder. 'Amit, if you're nervous, we can do this later. What I try to do is imagine a big red bin – it has to be red – and pulling all my nerves out of the top of my head and putting them in the bin, then putting the lid on.'

'You gay,' I said.

Mentally, though, I was extracting my nerves into Nishant's big red bin.

'Run it Dangerous. Let's do it!' I opened my mouth up wide. I jumped up and down. I was ready.

Nishant pressed 'record'. There was the slightest pregnant pause and he placed the needle delicately on the vinyl. Warmness, fuzziness, crackle and fiz . . .

BOOM BAP BOOM BOOM BAP
BOOM BAP BOOM BOOM BAP
BOOM BAP BOOM BOOM BAP
BOOM BAP BOOM BOOM BAP

Dangerous drops the beat, I drop heat
Like a pile of burning spaghetti on your white sheets
You Ku Klux Klan motherfucker
I get you down like a dead trucker
YOU CHUMP, I GOT YOUR RUMP

You're in luck, chump,
I saw her rump, it's mine first

I got the taste, I got the thirst, I'm about to burst
I get you down like a dead trucker
You're in luck, chump, I saw her rump, it's mine first
YEAAAAAAH

I got the taste, I got the thirst, I'm about to burst
You're the worst, you wear white shirts
When I hear the cops coming, I splurt
I got the planz, I got the gunz, I got the gunz and planz
Bring your manz, I spray them with fake tan
Blood coloured, you're dead like Mother Hubbard
I lock you in the closet, come out the cupboard
COCONUT COCOCOCOCONUT CITAAAY

This is Coconut Unlimited bringing the noise not the hype
Holding gunz to your head, hope you know your blood type
WE GOT THE GUNZ [GUNZZZZZ]
WE GOT THE PLANZ [MAAAAAN]
WE TAKE YOU OUT [YEEEEEAAAAAHHHHH]
THIS IS OUR LAND [COCONUT CITY]

Sit on your butt, sit on your rump, I take your girl
Out for ice cream, this is my world
I drop coconuts on your small dicky dick
Shove bums in your face for you to licky lick
I'm not gay, I'm built that way, you gotta pay me
I keep you throbbing like chocolate praline
I got gunz and planz, you like manz
I got chump change vans, I got alligator hands
Dangerous drops the beat like a baby
MC AP start taking all your ladies
With the one Mit Dogg I bring the streets back
I know how to do it, I got the knack
Born in the ghetto where life is tough
I had to be the roughest of the rough
Now I'm smooth like butter, thick like trees
Taking all your guns and moneys with ease

116

WE GOT THE GUNZ [GUNZZZZZ]
WE GOT THE PLANZ [MAAAAAN]
WE TAKE YOU OUT [YEEEEEAAAAAHHHHH]
THIS IS OUR LAND [COCONUT CITY]

It sounded amazing. Fierce, pumped and full of energy, and even though you could only hear the vocals in one ear and everytime Anand did a backing vocal it made the instrumental track go distorted and fuzzy, and you could hear Nishant falling into the pool table attempting a 360 degrees spin two minutes in, it sounded amazing. It was so good we bumped it up to track one of 'Coconut Unlimited Mixtape vol. 15 – We Got the Gunz We Got the Planz'. That first listen back was electric. We weren't really listening to the mix or checking it sounded OK. We were so hyped we were all singing along at top volume. Then Auntie Naina, Nishant's cheerful mum, knocked on the door and informed us that our dolphin-friendly tuna and sweetcorn toasted sandwiches were ready.

Success in my veins, I called a break.

*　　*　　*

We didn't see Herman's transformation coming. We were too 'rapped' up in rehearsing our set for the open mic and getting feedback for the one song we'd made, and for the mixtape too – a collection of all our favourite songs bundled onto a C-90 tape and ending with us all shouting: 'COCONUT UNLIMITED FOR EVER . . . SMOOTH LIKE BUTTER . . . DON'T YOU MUTTER . . . COCONUT UNLIMITED FOR–EVER–EVER–EVER.'

We gave Herman the first one and told him it was a freebie so he could go tell all his friends. We were selling them for £5, or £3 if you asked nicely. Or £2 if you drove a hard bargain. Or £1 if you had some social standing and our status would benefit from your patronage. Or free if you had loads of social standing and our status would increase Googleplex from your patronage.

We sold no tapes.

'Herman's probably just dubbing them for his mates,' Anand decided.

'Or he felt they wouldn't really be into it, so hasn't bothered.' Nishant said, ever the diplomat.

'Of course he was into it. He just . . . I don't know . . . people in this school have funny tastes.' I couldn't accept he hadn't passed our music on.

'CHUCKLES!' My moniker reverberated around the chemistry lab. I looked up at BS bashing a whiteboard pen against his forehead. 'All I can hear is bud–bud–bud–bud–bud–bud–bud–bud–bud–bud–bud–bud–bud–bud–bud–bud–bud–bud–ding–ding bud–bud–bud–bud–bud from you. Shut up or you can meet me after school, scrape off all the chewing gum from under my beautiful tables and chew it for the rest of your detention.'

'Sorry, Sir.'

Nishant put his hand up. BS tutted and pointed at him.

'What?'

'Sir, did you know that bud–bud ding–ding is considered offensive and racist?'

'Pardon? What? All I can hear is bud–bud–bud–bud–bud–bud–bud–bud–bud–bud–bud–bud. Now shut up!'

He turned back to the board. I heard Ahmed tut behind me. He acknowledged me in chemistry, physics and biology as we were setted in the middle set while Jasel and Pentil were in the upper echelons of advanced. He cut a solitary figure, craving companionship, but I wasn't ready to give it to him yet.

*   *   *

The lunch room was bustling. After weeks of quiet while the cool kids retired to the lake for a lickle smokey-smokey, they were now gathered in a corner of the room away from the serving abbatoirs of food, crowded around a happening. Anand, Nishant and I were at the edge of the crowd trying to peer in. There was a hush, and then . . . in the middle of the crowd, loudly and confidently with a hint of poshness . . .

> *I get money like banks, I'm hip deep in skanks*
> *I'm yo moma's loverman like my name was Shabba Ranks*
> *Guilty as charged, I got steel like tanks,*
> *While you off throwing shapes like yo name was Carlton Banks*
> *I'm a real big baller, got money in the piles*
> *I'm-a make you scream "OH MY GOD" like Joey Styles*
> *My secret's best kept, you're the clown in a dress*
> *I'm-a leave you holding up the wall like my name was Fred West*

There was applause, the crowd parted and then, pushing through them, appeared Herman. Looking all cool. Herman, the guy with fuzz all over his cheeks and a monobrow, white flakes whisping out of his scalp, tall and wirey and always tilting forwards awkwardly. *That* Herman. Yeah that one. People were cheering and patting him on the back. He emerged, saw me and Nishant and Anand, and pointed at us.

'Alright guys! Did you like my thing? I'm called Verbal Sharkey . . . you know, like Fergal Sharkey? But Verbal. Geddit?'

'Yeah,' I said, nonchalant.

'Thanks for the tape. There was some weird thing at the start with some weirdos shouting over that Nas instrumental but after that all the other tunes were badness. Luckily it was just one ear, so I turned the right speaker off and practised rapping on my own. What did you think? Who are they anyway?'

'Some local boys . . . Coconut Unlimited.' Much as it hurt to play it down, I still tried to be nonchalant.

'Oh right, not heard of them . . . '

'You will,' Nishant reassured him.

'I'm just gonna pass a hat round and get some change. I reckon I could make money from this. Listen, can you make me another tape, but with more instrumentals?'

'For free?' I asked, burning and burned. He'd cussed us.

119

I headed to the lunch serving area with flared nostrils, tense shoulders and a hankering for guilty chilli con carne, the self-hating Hindu's meal of choice.

Nishant patted me on the back. 'Don't worry, Amit. It's just one opinion . . . '

*　　*　　*

I sat in my bedroom playing and replaying 'We Got the Gunz We Got the Planz'. What was Herman's problem? It sounded awesome. I was in time with the beat, Anand sounded fierce and the instrumental was by Nas – what wasn't to love? I couldn't believe it.

The phone rang, and I heard Nish pick it up. She knocked on my door.

'COCONUT!' she shouted. 'ASH!'

Ash? What? Why is he calling me? How the hell did he have my phone number? That familiar heartbeat of thunder nerves began throbbing at my ribcage door. I cleared my throat to make sure I didn't sound meek.

'Wha gwarn?' I mocked up some confidence for my greeting.

'Yes, Amit. Whaa gwidarn, seen? Cool?'

'Seen, yeah, safe.'

'I need to see you.'

'Right, OK . . . '

'Come find me in the arcades.'

'I'm free tomorrow after school or Saturday.'

'You stupid Hindooo, I mean *now*. I'll see you in 15 or I'll come looking for you in 20. Round your mum's house.'

'I'm on my way.'

This presented me with a serious problem. It was 9.30 p.m., on a Monday. There was no way Mum was going to accept me heading out to St George's, especially to go see Ash. She knew of him and was glad I kept away. I was supposed to be doing my chemistry notes too.

Ash was waiting for me, though. If I didn't go, he'd come and get me and my mum would know we knew each other.

I put my shoes on and grabbed a coat, heading downstairs. I could hear the pressure cooker and the bud–bud chatter of Sunrise Radio in the kitchen. I poked my head round the door.

'What's up Mum?'

'Nothing is up. Vhy must something be up? Nothing is up. Talk to me properly.'

'I'm just popping out,' I said quickly, ducking back out the door fast, like pulling a plaster off – grip and yank. She looked up from rolling the chapatis.

'Popping ouvt? Vhere are you going? To see the bevakoof and the pendoo?'

'No Mum, Ahmed's house. He accidentally took some of my chemistry notes and I need them for my homework.'

She tutted and threw down her rolling pin. 'Vhy are you not careful? Vhy are you finding this oouvt nowv? Come, I will drivwe you.'

'No, no, it's fine Mum, you make tomorrow's chapatis. I'll walk. I need the fresh air. Actually, I'll run. Get the exercise . . . '

'It vill take two minutes, boyo, and you can be back to finish homevork qvicker. It's 9.30 p.m. You shouldn't still do homevork. This is relax time . . . '

'It's fine Mum. I want the fresh air.'

'Tho thel piva ja!' [Go and drink some oil!]

The walk to Harrow was ten minutes of winding through rows of terraced two-storey houses, all with the same façade: grey pebble-dash, white PVC doors and gravelled driveways. I always wondered what Indians had against grass and gardening because there wasn't a tuft of green anywhere in sight. The windows were garlanded with OM or swastika stickers. The cars were Nissan Micras for the girls and Mercedes for the boys. The broken pavement slabs, where I avoided the cracks, just in case, could've swallowed me up or split to unveil the tentacles of anxiety rising up to swallow me.

121

I could see the aquamarine dome of St George's and my chest pounding fell out of sync with the burn-burn of my stomach, two arrthymic gloryholes of destruction trying to kill me.

What did Ash want? Until a few months ago I had nothing to do with him save for the occasional hello, and that was usually when he strutted past and you couldn't help but stare and he'd turn to acknowledge you. Now, it seemed, I was his go-to guy and it was mildly disconcerting. No, it was incredibly disconcerting.

I arrived at the side entrance of St George's and peered in. Downstairs was mostly empty except for the escalators, which were ferrying everyone up to the arcades or cinema. Come on, I thought, there are times in your life when you've got to stop worrying and walk up to someone and let them say what they want to say. I pulled open the door. Some syrupy r'n'b was oozing out of the speakers. Why did Asians love r'n'b so much? They weren't particularly sexual people. They were scared of black people. They had no soul. It angered me so much. Sexy r'n'b had its place, but it wasn't with me, and I didn't understand my people's affinity for it and how they could listen to it in tandem with bhangra and Bollywood.

The escalator was filled with rudeboys and their gyals.

The boys: gelled spiky hair in a variety of angles and shaved sides, jumpers with logos emblazoned near their nipples, Moschino or Ralph Lauren or Armani – s'all bout da laaaaabels blud – jeans with insignias all over them, gleaming white trainers, gold rings on every finger displaying religious iconography.

The girls: grey or green contact lenses, foundation like paté, catty eye make-up and the rest all in black, their long small fingernails painted golden, their hair straight and middle-parted, small, all under five-foot – all so generic, so exactly the same that there was nothing even remotely attractive about them.

The escalator reached the top. I was deposited in front of Woolworths and saw, to my left, Ash leaning against the entrance

122

to the arcade, nodding up and down at me repeatedly and looking at his watch. He clapped. I smiled nervously and walked towards him, purposeful. He didn't need to know how scared I was.

'Hi Ash.'

'Young pup, you cool? Shall we go get a beer?'

'I'm cool. I gotta get back . . . '

'Dawg, I've bought you a beer. Come.'

He led me back into the arcade, striding ahead towards a table by the bar. Two Budweiser bottles were on the table. He sat down. I sat down. He looked at me and grabbed the beer, downing nearly half of it.

'Help yourself bro. This ain't no special occasion or nothing.'

I was panicking. I mean, what was in the bottle? I hadn't seen it being opened. There could be anything in it. Someone could've spat in it. Someone could've slipped some drugs into it. That's what we were told to expect, right, at drugs talks at school? Always be wary of bottles and cans you haven't opened yourself in case they've been spiked. What if one sip of this beer sent me into a loop of insanity and craziness and I couldn't make it stop? I was worried.

'Drink it for fuck's sake.'

'Man, I can't . . . I'm allergic.'

'To beer?' He laughed. 'You pussy . . . allergic to beer. What a prick.'

'Actually, I am.' I was indignant. Yeah you're scary, Ash, but I choose not to drink. I choose to worship my body. 'I nearly died once. It's a really serious allergy so I don't think it's funny. You can laugh all you want but you're laughing about me nearly dying.'

'What do I give a toss about your allergies man?'

'Sorry, Ash.'

'Sorry sorry sorry – look, I'm gonna get straight to the point of the case, the crucial elements of the conversation, for your perspiration, right? Listen, them boys at that private school of yours, they're bumming me. They're bumming me in the shitter and you know what? I don't like being bummed in the shitter and you know why? I ain't gay, ya get me? Seen? I ain't gay but they want to make me their battyman. So, I need you to go sort it out. Let these honky milk bottle motherfuckers and that Bounty boy Jasel know. I gots my manz on the inside, seen? You're my man on the inside, right?'

'Ash, I can't get involved . . . '

'You can't get involved? You *are* involved. This is your deal. You made this happen.'

'All I did was introduce two people . . . '

'That's the definition of a deal.' He had this knowing smirk, the corners of his mouth curled in victory.

'Then why didn't I get any money?' I murmured, frustrated, worried. This was getting too big for me.

'Money? Ha! Is that what this is about little man? You want payment for your services and then we can go on to the next services? I thought your rich honky bredrin would've sorted you out. But obviously not. Nah, cool. I'll do it.' He pulled out a wad of fivers, crinkled, and some twenty pence pieces fell to the floor. He got down to pick them up. The tension dipped.

'I don't want money Ash,' I said quietly, looking at the entrance, which was my exit.

'You need to man up. This is your shit-uation. You be handling it.'

'Ash, I . . . '

'You know what happened to the last boy that mugged me off? I gave some bre'er some deep psychological shit with a baseball bat to his face cos I was wearing shorts one day and we woz at them urinals and some of his piss spray went on my leg. My leg, little man. Don't be piss spray or I'll fuck you up.' He pulled his face in close. 'You *will* do this for me.'

'What are they up to?' I asked meekly, my resolve crumbling.

'This business is all about accountability and accounting you know? I give them some stuff and they give me some money and they're walking around in the latest garms when I know the product they're selling should be giving them enough for last season's at the most, you know? So, the question is, how have they got more than they should? I want to see some accounts or some receipts or something.'

I had no idea what he was talking about.

'You're gonna be my watchful eye. And everytime they got new garms and new kicks and new ting-a-lings, you're going to write them down in a notebook, with the style number, colour, approximate cost and make and then in a month's time I'll review the findings, and we'll make our move from there. OK?'

'Yeah . . . ' I still didn't know what he was talking about but I just wanted to get away. Mum might be phoning to check I got to where I said I was going. She knew where I kept the school Blue Book.

'I *will* be checking on you.'

He backed away and I turned to leave.

'I'm gonna tell you this straight right?' he said, grabbing my own before I could get away. 'I know you wanna be a rap star and you're all rugged and shit, mincing about like you superstars, but you know what? The white man owns the world. The white man runs tings propa in dis place and you're their pussyhole till you man up and take the power. See this white boy in school, I don't even know man's name. I know his face and I know his arse but to me he's just a white man who ain't worthy of my knowing his name so I just call him Honk-Honk. I got the power. He may be rich, but I own his arse. I beg you do the same. You're a proud Hindu warrior, now go out there and mash it up bredrin. Safe?' He held his fist out for a bump. I bumped it silently with a goofy 'I don't know how to respond' grin on my pie-hole.

'Safe,' I murmured.

'I can't hear you.'

'Safe,' I said, a bit louder.

'Pardon?'

'SAFE!' I shouted. A few heads turned round at my voice.

He pointed towards the door. It was time for me to leave.

I walked home tracing back the words in my head, with its platter of nonsensities. My journey was fraught with more cracks in the pavement. The crumbling concrete of a 70s obsession with new office blocks, now deserted by their occupants for the centre of London, was an apt metaphor for my Harrow(ing) state of mind.

*   *   *

Anand and Nishant found me drowning my sorrows in two Kit-Kats in the school tuck shop, charmingly called The Lun.

'We got a bit of a problem,' Nishant said, vibrating.

My mind was elsewhere. Anand already knew the problem. I was playing catch-up the apathetic way.

I didn't look at him. I was watching Pentil and Jasel heading towards the lake. I was trying to see what trainers they had on; black ones obviously, a loophole in the uniform and dresscode that insisted footwear (not qualifying shoes but leaving it open to accidentally include trainers) be black or brown.

'I was talking to Eddy this weekend and he was saying that the open mic doesn't have a record player there. I mean, what am I going to do? I don't know how to play the music.'

I snapped out of it. 'What? What do you mean there's no decks. What kind of open mic is this?'

'Yeah, exactly.'

'What are we going to do? We need a solution . . . '

Anand looked up. 'Oh, we've got one.'

'What's that?' I was slipping.

'Well, we play the song off a tape recorder belonging to the sound man – Eddy said there'll be a soundman who'll play our music for us – then we do the song and Nishant does some dancing in the background . . . '

'Nah, boo dat, man, who wants to see some rugged urban streetwise rappers and a dancer?'

'We should do a song called "Streetwise",' Nishant said, nodding.

'Nah,' Anand persisted. 'It's not just dancing. It's breakdancing.'

'What's breakdancing?' I asked.

'Like the stuff that invented hip-hop. Like b-boys.'

I'd heard reference to breaking and b-boys and stuff on rap songs. Maybe this was what they meant.

'Can you do any breakdancing?' I asked Nishant.

'Well, I taped this thing on Channel 4 last night. I'll learn it. Plus, they do breaking in this car park behind the civic centre.'

'Do they?'

'Yeah, Eddy told me.'

'When did you guys see Eddy?' I said, hurt.

'On Saturday. We called you but no one answered the phone.'

'I thought you guys were busy this weekend . . . '

'I was free,' said Anand.

'Yeah, and we didn't go to the exhibition in the end because Mum felt it was an embarrassing example of fascistic tendencies,' Nishant said. 'So we went Harrow.'

'Yeah. Saw Eddy. Saw Ash. He was asking for you. Nishant gave him your number . . . '

'What? Why?'

'Cos he scares me,' said Nishant.

'Why? Did he call you?'

'Yeah, he did . . . '

I was reticent about Ash with these guys because they feared him, and they had every right to. At the same time, these bozos were my bozos and they were my spars. I loved them.

So I told them everything.

Nishant's reaction was to marvel at how much this felt like a cop thriller. After dismissing him, I asked Anand what to do. He shrugged.

'You do what Ash asks. You always do.' He looked so serious. I was worried about getting caught and accused of being a drug pusher or smoker myself. Anand, pragmatic for once, told me that all I'd be doing was watching people for people. I wasn't touching anything, I wasn't taking anything. My hands were clean. I just needed to keep my distance from Ash.

'Shall we follow them down now and see?' Nishant was excited at the prospect of espionage.

'Nishant . . . '

'Nah man, leave him,' Anand said, standing. 'We got your back. We Coconuts forever, still.'

'Yeah,' Nishant affirmed, lightly touching Anand on the shoulder, chuffed he'd been stood up for.

'We'll come with you.'

'Thanks Dangerous, that's pretty cool, but shouldn't you be rehearsing?'

Nishant stopped, and looked confused.

'I mean, don't you have a dance to rehearse for Coconut Unlimited's first gig?' I smiled.

Nishant punched the air, a massive grin over his bed-head face, joy and rapture and happiness oozing through him like a slow-acting poisonous dart of pleasure.

'Yes!' he exclaimed, post-fist punching, as if its motion wasn't enough. 'Can I really?'

'Yeah man.'

Nishant ran off, excited.

'What we looking for then?' Anand asked, stepping closer.

I explained what Ash had demanded, as best I could.

'So they're buying weed off him and selling it right?' said Anand.

'Yeah.'

'And they're buying stuff with their money?'

'Yeah.'

'What does he care?'

'I don't know. But I'm not sure I want to find out . . . '

We wandered down to the lake, to where Pentil and Jasel held court, selling and smoking. The bushes and trees added enough foliage and the wind and water covered any clumsy stealth twigs we broke on our journey down.

It was the usual crew: Pentil, Jasel, some sixth formers, Pete Hall – the policeman's son, lost in his own sturdy world of make-believe and toxicated paranoia, fighting the lake with the hunting knife he had on him at all times. He was wild and erratic and full of surging bodily functions.

'They're wearing school uniform,' I whispered to Anand. 'There's no way of telling if they have new stuff,'

'Nah, look . . .' he said, pointing at Pentil's feet. 'Those are new kicks.'

'Are they?'

A loud noise caused us to scuffle, till we realised it was the boom and bellow of my nemesis, Herman.

Listen up, I smoke blunts and crack nuts . . .
You dumb bucks got straight shook up like George Lutz
Never step in my manor, I'm a dog with the big bite
Face it, you just Vanilla Ice – I'm Suge Knight
Cos I'm a big bad wolf, you a yappy little pooch
Put my trainer in your face, leave you looking like Hooch
I'll throw you to my dogs if you ever step to me
Why you even wanna try? I'm a flippin' Pedigree

He had his eyes closed, rapping away. Pentil and Jasel were standing around him, nodding.

'You should battle him Mit Dogg. Take him down.'

'Nah,' I twinged. 'He's not even on my radar yet blud.' He was amazing, but I wouldn't be caught admitting this. 'So, what trainers is them?'

'New Air Max. Version two or something. Black with white swoosh.'

'How new?'

'Dunno. He weren't wearing them a week ago.'

'Could he save up enough to buy them in a week?'

'From selling weed? Look at Pete, he looks like he buys in bulk.'

'True dat.' I looked over at the freak.

'Mit, check it . . . we do go to a private school . . . '

'And?'

'Well it's just a case of, "Yo Dad, gimme £100". And he'll be, like, "Sure, anything for the apple of my rich eye" and he won't even care what the bredda is spending it on!'

'Try telling Ash that.'

'That they're rich boys? They can afford all this stuff . . . '

'Yeah.'

'And you should tell him that this is a good market cos they can afford to buy loads, and don't mess it up. And tell him to leave you alone cos one word to Pentil and the business stops and that means the cash stops. Business means getting *paid*.'

I looked back at the guys. They were starting to disperse and heading back to school. There was nothing dodgy going on here, I decided.

I just had to explain that to Ash.

*   *   *

'There's nothing dodgy going on, man.' I squared my chest out in mock bravado. Ash was less than impressed. 'We all go to a rich private school, their parents can afford to buy them new trainers and jackets and garms. It doesn't mean they're ripping you off or whatever . . . '

'I know that, dickhead,' Ash bellowed. I looked round, worried that people were looking. 'That ain't why I got my secret squirrel Amizzle dizzle on the case. Didn't you listen to what mans said? I want you to note down everything they're wearing and I'll do the rest. I need to work out how much those garms all cost. Then I know how much they can afford. Then I can suddenly claim that there's some big weed drought and all the crops died, that I got a connect but it's more expensive. This is a business. A game. It's a game of business. And business is all about expansion. You tell me, what would you do?'

'With . . . ?'

'Dumbass, you got a private school full of potential stoners with enough daddy dollars to pay what you want. What do you do?'

'Dunno.'

'They don't teach you much about mass economic accumulatative speculation in that school do they? You make money-money, you take money-money. I'm charging them fuckers double. You're lucky I don't make you buy from me and sell it on.'

'Nah, cool man.'

'You ever smoked dat shit?'

'No man!' I said, disgusted, like he'd spat on my tongue.

'Accumulatative speculation bruv. You're a customer. And a middleman. And a brother . . . '

*　　*　　*

Anand's relationship with Meena had taken a strange and immasculating turn. They barely liked each other. Everytime she was around they had hissed arguments but we hardly saw her because she couldn't bear to be in the same room as us. She hated me and thought Nishant was a doofus, but she needed Anand. His thin short bony hips and flat chest gave him the perfect frame for a female model. Meena had dreams of designing sarees, mixing Western designs like tartan and tribal Maori patterns with Indian sequins – and who better to model the lime green and fluorescent yellow monstrosities than Anand and his slight frame. Anand insisted he be photographed from the neck down so his face was never visible, and she obliged. You'd never be able to tell it was him, he looked that much like a pigeon-chested teenage girl. But we knew.

She revealed his shame mid-argument one day when we were rehearsing. She'd wanted to go and sit in the park and he was choosing us over her. We were starting to sound like a proper band and even Nishant's breakdancing was coming along. We'd open the French doors over our studio rehearsal space, our 'Cocobunker', and carry the pool table outside so Nishant could pop and lock and spin on his head. Meena would sit upstairs in the kitchen and sketch new designs. Her new idea was to design sarees of female superheroes like She-Ra, or Cheetara from *Thundercats*, or *Wonder Woman*.

In terms of physical advancement, Anand hadn't progressed past kissing, light petting (under shirt/over bra) and dry-humping/thigh frottage. They never had an opportunity to be home alone together. Both lived in families with gentrified housewives home all the time, cooking, and traditional in their views on relationships: study till you have a job and, when you do, we'll find you a wife. Till then, your girlfriend is a nice fountain pen and your children are a bumper twenty-pack of ink cartridges. When they weren't both ensconced in domicile perma-presence, they were with us.

There was no way we weren't going to nail this open mic, though. All the others were going to look so whack, ya get me.

*   *   *

I needed new clothes for the gig. Specifically, I needed some non-stonewashed jeans and a T-shirt with a rap band on it. And a hat. And maybe a sew-on badge with a cannabis leaf on it. It was time to visit the bountiful city of London Town.

We went to London as a family about once a year, as a treat. It was around Christmas and Dad wanted to walk down Oxford Street and see how his company's products were being displayed in all the retail stores. We'd park up at Marble Arch and wander the length of Oxford Street, stopping in all the relevant shops he wanted to check out, allowing Nish a trip into a toy shop and me a trip into a music shop before reaching Leicester Square and going for dinner then a film at the Empire cinema. It was the only thing we did as a family, an acquiescence to the hidden agenda of self-congratulatory monitoring of clients and the way they handled Dad's product.

But that Christmas, I was in a tizz. *The Source* and *Hip-Hop*

Connection had given Tupac's *Thug Life* side-project a mediocre review but raved about some guy called Notorious B.I.G. His lyrics to a song called 'Juicy', featuring references to stuff I didn't know anything about, were *The Source's* featured lyrics of the month. But I wanted the Tupac album, the *Thug Life* album, despite the lacklustre reviews.

I held them both up in the Virgin Megastore, gauging the covers. *Thug Life* was all black with a stencilled logo declaring THUG LIFE on it. The first song was called 'Bury Me a G'. The Notorious B.I.G. one had a white cover with a baby with a big afro on it. 'How was that gangsta?' I wondered. I put the Notorious B.I.G. album down while Mum and Nish waited patiently by the door, Dad having already disappeared to John Lewis. The one time a year I could legitimately buy music, guilt-free . . . it was to be *Thug Life*.

Mum took it to the counter and I hovered near her in line. She read the song titles and looked up at me.

'You sure you vant to vaste your treat on this?'

'Yeah. It's not a waste of money. It's good.'

'It sounds too wiolent. Vhy must you buy something so wiolent?'

'Cos it's good?'

'They sound dangerous.'

'They are, Mum. That's the point.'

'Vhy must they celebrate their powerty and wiolent vays of making the money?' she asked, taking out her purse to pay.

'It's empowerment, Mum. The white man keeps them down and they have to pull together and be better than the white man.'

'There's no such thing as a vhite man.'

The assistant grinned at me. Mum paid.

The walk down Oxford Street continued. I held the tape in my jacket pocket and pulled it out occasionally to check the cover. It was beautiful. And it came Mum-approved. She told me not to show Dad.

We started to near the end of Oxford Street. I heard the crash and thud of drum'n'bass emerging from the downstairs of a shop called Mash and looked over, seeing all their hip-hop wear in the window, baggy jeans and the big basketball shirts with logos of grown dreadlocked men smoking spliffs on, and even a pink T-shirt with a gold chain drawn on it, with 'De La Soul' in big yellow letters.

'Mum, I need some jeans.'

'You don't need jeans.'

'I do. I'm too tall for these ones now.'

'Ve vill go to C&A in Harrow next weekend.'

'Nah, Mum. Look . . . ' I pointed to Mash. 'Give me some money and I'll go and get them in there. They're good. Designer. Also baggy so it'll take me longer to grow out of them. I'm saving you money.'

'You vant to buy baggy jeans like black boys?'

'Yeah, Mum.' I needed to go in alone so ignored the comment.

'How much jeans?'

'Like, fifty pounds?'

'Fifty pounds? Tharoo farigyu che? [Are you dizzy?] Fifty pounds? On jeans? Too much.'

'Mum, it's designer. I'll look good.'

'I don't care. You are not spending fifty pounds on jeans. Ve'll go C&A.'

'God Mum, you're so tight!'

'Come then, ve go in and look together then.'

'What? No!'

There was no way I wanted Mum to come into the shop with me. There was no way I wanted her to see what I had in mind. And there was just simply no way I wanted to be seen with her in a drum'n'bass-playing shop selling cool garms, in London of all places.

'Ve go inside.'

Mum palmed Nish off on my annoyed dad, whose idea of family time was being present in body but not necessarily in mind. She grabbed my hand to cross the road and led me into the belly of the beast, this shop Mash, blaring out a song called *Original Nuttah!* Some guy was screaming about bad boys in London and rudeboys in Brixton.

She scrunched her nose up at me and declared loudly, 'Vhat are they saying? Is it Ing-er-lesh?'

I shook my head. I didn't know the answer.

The shop was full of people in their twenties, all dressed in graff-inspired T-shirts, baggy jeans and shaved heads. They were all standing around, leaning on speakers. Upstairs was just two walls plastered with posters and flyers for nights advertising SOUL R'N'B, JUNGLE, HIP-HOP, RAP, all in areas of London I'd never heard of, albums I'd never heard of, spray cans and skate-boards and albums and rappers, lots of rappers. I looked at Mum, recoiling at the speed of the music. She strode up to one of the shop assitants, her hands on her hips like she was telling him off.

'Young man, vhere jeans? My son vants to buy jeans.' The guy looked at me and stifled a laugh. 'Come on, young man,' Mum continued. 'Don't be lazy. I vant to buy my son jeans. Look at me.' He turned back to her, his teeth biting down on his bottom lip. 'Vhere are they?'

'Downstairs, ma'am.' He smiled and winked at me. 'You need a hand, you call me. Only me. I'm your man.' He winked as we shuffled past; well, I shuffled and Mum, being short and fat, waddled. 'I'm your man,' he mouthed at me.

The second black man I'd ever spoken to and he was rinsing me, taking the piss. I needed to be out of here. I was wearing my navy blue duffle raincoat from school cos it was cold outside. I looked like a pussyhole.

Downstairs was even more frantic, the music even louder. Mum put her hands to her ears, slightly fearful of all these youthful boys with shaved heads and fashionable girls all decked in graffiti-inspired clothing, and the Nuttah music trepanning both our brains.

'SHOW ME JEANS!' she shouted, unnecessarily.

I looked round. I needed to get out of here but this was a cool discovery at the same time. What was worse? Five minutes of embarrassment for bringing my mum into the coolest shop in the world, or not shopping here and therefore potentially not being dressed to my full potential?

I scanned the jeans. Much as I liked the baggy jeans with logos of grown dreadlocked men smoking spliffs on them, I didn't need any more similarities between Ash and me being drawn, so looked for plainer but baggy jeans, or logos that involved the name of the designer like Karl Kani or Moschino. I fingered some jeans and picked them up. Mum stood in the middle of the shop floor, spinning round and slowly watching the crowd disapprovingly, her hands on her hips. I couldn't concentrate. I had no way of differentiating between good and bad jeans. I looked to see what others were wearing. Mum, with her hands on her hips, turned to look at my rabbit-lost face, bewildered by choice. She strode over, pulling the nearest jeans to us.

'This one?' She waved it at me, spun on her heel and accosted the nearest guy she could find. 'My son needs 32-30.'

'I don't work here Mummy darling,' said the guy. 'See my man over here.' She spun round and accosted another, demanding the same size from him. The music felt louder and faster. I shielded myself from the embarrassment. The guy walked over to where I was standing, holding out the jeans he'd been given.

'Here you go fella . . . these *are* 32–30.'

'Safe man.'

'You wanna try them on?'

'Yes, my son vishes to try them on. Vhere can he?'

'Right here Mama.' He led us along to the changing room.

'Mama? You call me Mama?' She entered the changing room with me. 'These kalas [black people] are friendly here . . . '

'Mum, what are you doing?'

She sat on the stool in the cubicle. 'Go on then, show me . . . '

'Mum, GET OUT!'

'What shame hawe you got? I'we seen it before . . . '

'This is private!'

She started to cry, holding her hands to her face. 'My son is so ungrateful. He thinks he can talk to his mother this vay. He thinks he is gora but dresses like kala. He hates his desi [brown people] ancestors. Vhy can I hawe son like Ravi? Good boy . . . respectful boy . . . '

'Mum, just stop crying, OK?'

'No, you talk to your mother properly and I stop crying.'

'Mum, please. I'm just, you know, embarrassed. I don't want you to see me naked . . . '

'Naked? You are wearing chudees [pants].'

'Yeah . . . '

'So vhat's problem? Show me expensive jeans . . . '

'Mum get out!'

She stood up and waved her arms, to show she was washing her hands of me.

'Tho thel piva ja maree su? [Go and drink oil what's it to me?] Come and show me expensive jeans vhen ready. I vait outside with the kalas.'

'Mum, shh!'

She walked out of the cubicle. I tried the jeans on and stared at myself in the mirror, my legs lost in swathes of gangsta blue denim, my white socks like rugs of insincerity in the most amazing jeans ever. I needed to sell this to Mum. I needed these jeans badly. I needed to convince her that they weren't a waste of money, but instead the one thing I could help her save money on in the long run, when actually what I was doing was increasing my social stature about tenfold. I looked at the price. They were £27. Interesting, nearly half the price I'd told her when she'd come into the shop with me. I walked out.

She was next to the shop assistant.

'Looking bad-ass, Mr Amit.' He winked at my mum, who had

the smile of someone who needed to dress up what she really thought with empty platitudes.

'Vell they fit you.'

'Yeah that's the style Jayu,' the guy told Mum. What had they been talking about? 'It's all about the baggy look. It's very American.'

'You are very sweet Tito,' she said, smiling at him. 'I've never met such a gorgeous boy like you. They usually hang around Harrov vith kniwes and guns and who knows what else.'

'Listen, Mama. I'm gonna let that slide because you might buy these jeans for your young man and he's going to look tight, and I work on commission. Otherwise, we'd be having words.'

Awkward pause, then he laughed and she laughed with him. I wasn't sure if she knew what he was actually saying.

'Sorry man, my mum, you know . . . she's sheltered. I'm in a hip-hop band . . . '

'It's cool man. She's old school, I get that – plus, I really do work on commission. Hip-hop band, eh? They discovered rap along with indoor plumbing up in Bumville, Middlesex?'

'TITO!' Mum scolded, giggling. Oh my God, she thought he was flirting with her. 'Language!"

'Sorry, Mama. Listen, Amit, you look tight. You look loose. You're buying those jeans.'

I looked at Mum. She looked at Tito and giggled. The garms were mine.

'Now, Amit, you need accessories. Hip-hop is all about accessories. It's all about looking like a bad boy. What else can we get you?'

Then I saw it . . . up on the wall . . . a hat with Dr Dre's logo on it. Well, it wasn't a hat. It was a long sock with a big green cannabis leaf and 'Dr Dre' written in some graffiti gothic script over the top. The long sock was wide enough to fit over my head and it was tied with a lace at one end. It was supposed to droop over the back of your head. Or the side. This was proper gangsta-wear. You could imagine a guy with an AK-47 wearing the hat and the jeans with gleaming orange Timberland boots on his feet.

'How much is the Dre hat?' I asked nonchalantly. Inside, I was bursting with complete happy tingling brilliant glowing amazingness.

'Fiver, mate.'

'I'll take three.' I looked at Mum. 'For Anand and Nishant's Christmas present . . . ' Then I nodded to Tito. 'For my crew, na'meen?'

*   *   *

Non-uniform day arrived and I was ready. I got up half an hour early, checked out the carpet man I had dressed on the floor, dusted off each garment with care love and attention and hit the shower. To look good, I needed to smell good and to smell good, I needed some manly shower gel. I washed, nodded to my bemused dad on the way back to my bedroom and saw him on the floor: me, but with no body, just empty clothes awaiting skin and bones.

I started with the jeans, the baggy Bleubolt jeans with pockets near the backs of the knees; not too much detail, but much bagginess. I felt awesome and stared at myself in the mirror, ignoring the puppy fat of my man boobs, the inconsistent sprouts of hair fuzz and the belly button shaped like the saggy jowls of Richard M. Nixon. I pursed my lips, threw up a gun hand towards the mirror and, hearing the imaginary beat, spouted off some new lyrics for the Coconuts.

> *I bring it bad and gutter, don't mutter, you utter berk*
> *I make your girls so horny they give me a circle jerk*
> *I lurk in most places, have most faces, on a daily basis*
> *And no I don't like white boy shit like Oasis, no way sis . . .*

I heard a bang and smack on the mutual wall with my sister, and shut up. It was still early. But hot damn, I looked fit in these jeans. I was considering hitting up Harrow afterwards, just to gauge the attention. I picked up my De La Soul T-shirt with the

139

yellow medallion logo and slipped it on. I caught myself in the mirror and whispered the rest of the verse.

> *I get badder and badder, you get fatter*
> *Stop eating pies, your health matters*
> *I splatter you with your own blood and viscous*
> *I kill your wife like my name was Sid Vicious*

I pulled up my sleeveless puffa jacket. It was like a bulletproof vest in *Boyz n the Hood*, then picked up the cannabis leaf brooch that I'd got for 50p at Mash, when I'd claimed to have forgotten the receipt in the shop and my dad, the accountant, had insisted I go back to reclaim it for tax purposes. This was solely for the procurement of a metallic brooch, which was shaped like a cannabis leaf with deceptively sharp leaf-ends, and pinned to your jacket.

I didn't tell Mum about that bit. She was still lording over me that she'd spent money on new clothes when they could barely afford to pay for food. The business was doing badly and they still had to pay for my schooling. Dad tutted at her and said a treat now and then was good for morale. He saw this as a bribe for me to work harder on coursework. I was his little investment for the future.

I held on tight to the bag of jeans, only ordered a starter and drank tap water to atone for making Mum spend money on me. I looked at my stupid sister, burning with jealousy. I got the private education, I got the new jeans and I got new music all because I was firstborn son. She was nothing less than a perfect Gujarati daughter and what did it get her? A childhood of sexist austerity. She hated my guts. And that made me feel good.

Once the cannabis brooch was safely on and I was looking suitably bad-ass in the mirror, I picked up the Dr Dre sock hat and placed it on my head, trying to get the flappy top bit, the bit tied with thread, to rest somewhere cool. If it went to the back, it stretched over the Dr Dre bit. If it went to the side, you could see the whole of the Dr Dre logo but the thread tickled my cheek. So be it, I decided. It was time to look bad-ass now.

I waited till Dad was out of the bathroom and there was the

window where he switched on the television and got changed, and Mum woke up to the headlines and nothing else in the house was stirring, then I ran downstairs, grabbing some crisps and a can of Coke for breakfast and shouting that I'd make my own way home this evening.

I headed out the door, winded up the suburban streets of my home town and zeroed in on school, knowing I'd eventually catch up with Anand and Nishant and we three would have our matching hats. Freedom tasted amazing. It tasted of deep-fried potato snacks and miscellaneous fizzy drink. It tasted of making my own way to school, a battle I was slowly winning against my overbearing mum and dad. All I needed now was a quicker way to get there, because much as I wanted to make it there by myself it was about twenty minutes walk to Anand and Nishant's houses, and they had a twenty-five minute walk to school from there. Forty-five minutes was bare long, ya get me, especially when it was ten minutes in the car on Dad's way to work.

I started to walk faster towards their houses. They knew to be waiting for me. I tried not to walk too quickly in case the sweatiness of my upper body, caused by the unnecessarily-warm-for-this-time-of-year puffa waistcoat, started to override my deodorant and made me smell like the rest of the scummy rich boys at school.

I reached Ash's house, lifeless and quiet, then Ahmed's house, which looked bustling, but I hurried, feeling the familiar sting of his betrayal in my stomach. I walked straight through St George's to the other side. I was cooking now, nearing Nishant's house. We were meeting there and then we'd listen to a Nas song together, and head out in our new hats, looking *pretty cool*.

Walking through the school gates and seeing everyone in their non-uniform alter-egos was weird. We didn't socialise outside of school. They certainly didn't socialise with us either so seeing them all dressed in non-uniform versions of themselves was a surprising mix of khaki, shirt and jumper combos for the rich-rich kids, and Rage Against the Machine T-shirts for the rebellious ones.

I reliably saw Jasel as one of the khaki and shirt boys, a preppy extension of the man he professed to be, almost indentikit with Pentil who'd eschewed last year's Nine Inch Nails rebellion for a more 'smart casual' look. Ahmed was generically daubed in white T-shirt and jeans, not pushing any boats anywhere.

And then we unleashed ourselves through the front gates, looking mega awesome sauce. Anand was wearing his XL white T-shirt, some baggy jeans he'd got off his fatter dad with a belt holding them up and his Nike Air sneaks. And the hat. Nishant had on a T-shirt he'd found in a market with a breakdancer on it, his white tennis shoes, black jeans . . . and the hat. I didn't mind him looking slightly different because he looked hard in black.

We strutted the two hundred metres up the school drive, past the rugby pitches and into the heart of the school. People were doing that thing of whispering about us through the sides of their mouths. Some were laughing. Most were astonished. No one could touch us. Electric boogaloo.

The end of the drive where the path suddenly ploughed a rough and ready trajectory into school was littered with crisp packets and rebellious cigarette butts. We strode down, mostly in silence, bopping along to our internal beats, ready for the onslaught.

Except, when we got to my classroom, a scary problem presented itself. There was safety in Coco-numbers but, while Anand and Nishant were in the same classes for the rest of the day, I was by myself. Anand patted me on the back and told me I'd be fine.

We dapped fists and they disappeared down the corridor. I pushed my classroom door open, expecting chaos. There was a hush as I walked in. BS was standing up, his hands on his hips, a rugby top and shorts wrapped round his bulky muscular frame. Everyone was attentively looking at him. I checked my watch. I was early. What the what?

'Oh, don't worry . . . you're not late . . . ' he said, smiling. 'Black Beauty . . . '

There was a ripple of laughs. I looked round the room for help.

The laughter went up a notch.

'NEEEEEEEEEEEIIIIIIIIIGGGGGGGGGGGGHHHHHHHHHH!' erupted from Pentil's desk and Jasel got up, bounding down the aisle like he was on a horse. Pentil grabbed the other aisle.

BS kept his eyes on me, grinning. 'Dear Chuckles,' he said. 'What a picture you do paint, my boy. Why? You're dressed like Black Beauty. Come and sit here.' He pointed to a chair next to his desk. I muffled forward and slowly sat down next to him while the NEIGHing and BRAYing simmered down. 'Right,' he declared. 'It has been brought to my attention that there is unsavoury prejudice in this school and I'm going to get to the bottom of it. Some people think, young Black Beauty, that you're mocking poor black ghettoes in America with your taste in music and clothes and I want us all to role-play this – get to the bottom of it. You, my boy, need to decide whether you want to be black . . . or brown, like you were born to be. If you want to be brown and yourself, well, there's no helping you. If you're trying to convince us all you want to be black, then my boy, I believe you might be due a literal dressing down.'

'Sir, I . . .'

'Shut up, Chuckles . . . ' He stopped, zeroing in on my cannabis leaf brooch. He pointed to it. 'Chuckles, do you know what this leaf does to a man?'

'Yes, Sir.'

'Are you aware of the legal implications of being caught tampering with this leaf?'

'Yes, Sir.'

'Have you ever smoked this leaf?'

'No, Sir.'

'Do you know anyone who has?'

'No, Sir.' I made sure I eyeballed a red-eyed Pentil at this point.

'Why wear it?'

'I like the way it looks.'

'Despite the legal ramifications?'

143

'Yes, Sir.'

I got up and went to my desk, the Dr Dre hat flaccid in my hand. The neighing was a slow humming murmur behind and around me. BS sat down at his desk, fumbled a pencil into his oversized meat-hands, looked down his Roman nose at me with those impenetrable grey eyes and started marking the register. I put the Dr Dre hat in my bag.

The rest of the day was a blur of chaos as everyone slipped into their outside personas, happy to be in plain clothes and thus able to suitably mock each other for their fashion cases. When I caught up with Anand and Nishant, they were still defiantly rocking their hats.

'Where's your hat?'

'Oh, I took it off. It was hot in class.'

'Everyone's been saying our hats are weird,' Nishant said. 'I made sure I kept it on so they know what we're talking about.'

'Peoples just don't know, they don't understand.' Anand was firm, stronger than me, still hatted. 'You should put your hat back on.'

'Nah, it's OK guys, seriously. I'm too hot.'

'Come on, Mit Dogg, Coconut Unlimited is a team and you're our leader,' Nishant implored.

I smiled. I loved that goofy boy. I pulled my hat out of the bag, grinning, and fixed it on my head.

It was lunchtime. We strutted down the corridor in arrow formation. Nishant practiced the odd 360 degree twirl, Anand had his gun fingers on standby and I had the lazy dragging leg behind me. We looked awesome. We ignored the calls of 'BLACK BEAUTY' and the neighing. We just listened to the beats in our head. I was listening to 'Don't Believe the Hype' by Public Enemy, remembering why I loved this music, remembering that I was an oppressed minority just trying to get by, by any means necessary, and remembering that I was in an awesome rap group and these losers knew nothing about the spirit and camaraderie of hip-hop. BLAM.

The lunchroom was humming louder than the cascades of fading pisstake references to our political blackness. I could hear the familiar rapping of one Mark Herman, aka Verbal Sharkey. The plan was to get in and get our lunch while they were all distracted. We headed in. Herman was mid-flow. They all stopped looking at him and pointed at us, laughing hysterically. Soon the entire right-wing of the lunchroom was screaming 'BLACK BEAUTY' at us, again and again, and there was nothing for it. I'd had enough.

'Verbal . . . ' I shouted over the din.

[BLACK BEAUTY BLACK BEAUTY]

'Yes, Amit . . . how you doing man? You cool? Sorry about all this, it'll die down.'

[BLACK BEAUTY BLACK BEAUTY]

'We're battling.'

[BLACK BEAUTY BLACK BEAUTY]

'What's that?'

[BLACK BEAUTY BLACK BEAUTY]

'Like rap battles . . . rhyming battle to see who's best!'

[BLACK BEAUTY BLACK BEAUTY]

'Oh right . . . do we have to?'

[BLACK BEAUTY BLACK BEAUTY]

'It's the spirit of hip-hop.'

[BLACK BEAUTY BLACK BEAUTY]

'Oh in that case . . . '

[BLACK BEAUTY BLACK BEAUTY]

'Everyone SHUT THE FUCK UP!'

'Right, Amit and I . . . '

'Mit Dogg . . . '

'Sorry, now Mit Dogg and Verbal Sharkey are going to do a rap battle to see who's got the best spirit of hip-hop.' There were some titters, some stunned silence, a lot of smug smiles. 'Mit, why don't you go first so I know what it is . . . ?'

'Safe blaaaad.'

I looked him up and down. I checked out his acne, his height, the uneven way he let his fingernails grow. I checked out what school house he was in and ran through the different ways I could humiliate their sporting achievements. I checked out his voice, what subjects he was best at. Why did Herman have to be such a stand-up guy? The silence was like vinyl crackle, loud and imposing. Someone punctuated it with a quiet 'NEIGH' so I squared him down and launched into my battle rap . . .

YEEEEEEEEEEEEEAAAAAAAAAAHH
HHHHHHHHHCOCONUTUNLIMITED
LISTEN
LISTEN
Listen
Listen
Yo, so Herman's a munster, his mum's a munter
Down the market he's an ordinary punter
Who wants pizza? Herman's got a pizza face
Herman always loses a race
Err . . .
Listen
YEEEEEEEEEEAAAAAAAAAHHHHHHHHHH COCONUT
Herman, Herman, you're just a bit shit man
You got fingernails like you filed them with a flan
You can't rap, you're just crap
Who's with me, feel me, BRRAAP
Yap, clap trap, dapper . . .
Map . . . lap COCONUT UNLIMITED

I opened my eyes. Most people had drifted away leaving Herman, Anand and Nishant moshing to my words, Jasel and Pentil laughing and Ahmed standing idly by, eyeing up the bursting lunch queue with a few others. Herman looked at me.

'That was a bit mean . . .'

'That's how you prove your skills.'

'Is it? OK, I'll give it a go man.'

Mit Dogg, more like Shit Log
Take your skills outside into the thick fog
That your farting mouth just made
Look man, I'm getting paid and laid
And you're just a whack little man
Who can't rap, I'm like damn
Come on, these are the skills you're bringing
That's why everyday I'm winning . . .

Jasel and Pentil applauded wildly, causing some drifters to wander over and applaud for applauding's sake.

'Pre-written,' I murmured.

'What? No, come on Amit. I came up with those on the spot like you told me to. I didn't mean those things.'

'PRE-WRITTEN!' I shouted. 'PRE-WRITTEN PRE-WRITTEN PRE-WRITTEN.'

I grabbed some mash from a discarded plate nearby and flung it at Herman, running out of the lunchroom, stifling tears. I headed for the sanctuary of our empty classroom and sat in there by myself, staring at the clock and waiting for school to end. I even thought about calling Mum to pick me up, to avoid the walk home.

I thought about Herman too. Should I say sorry? He did beat me. He had skills, and I was a shit log.

Fifteen slow minutes later and Nishant and Anand meekly pushed through the door, clutching a grease-sodden lukewarm bag of chips for me from the tuck shop. Nishant held it out and I half-smiled, eating the hardened husks of deep-fry out of gratitude. We sat in silence while Nishant did some spins and some popping and locking, Anand stared into space and I concentrated on my chips.

The day dripped by like water torture, like leaky pipes, like ennui and silence. I spoke to no one and no one spoke to me for the rest of the day.

Next: Shit gets real

CHAPTER SIX

The Chronic

I'd missed my Thursday comics run for band practice, so there I was, Monday evening, out of sync with the world. I flicked through my list and went to scan the shelves for anything that looked interesting.

Someone tapped me on the shoulder, and I turned round. It was Herman.

'Hey man.'

'Wha gwarn.'

'Hey Amit. That was so cool today. The battle. I really liked it. We should do more. Listen, next time, let's just do it by ourselves. Like, I think we were both nervous cos we were surrounded by people and I couldn't think that fast. Could you?'

'Nah man, it's, like . . . I was just, you know . . . in a bad mind after all that "Black Beauty" stuff. Next time, I'll take you.'

'Well, let's just practise. Maybe we should do a band together? There's an open mic at the Fat Controller we could go to when we're ready. It'd be great.'

'Man's got a band, Herman. Ya get me? Coconut Unlimited?' No way, I was thinking. Coconut Unlimited was my only love.

'*You're* Coconut Unlimited? I see now. That makes a lot of sense. I applaud your efforts, especially on the mixtape. Maybe we should pool together and get a four-track tape recorder and record stuff properly, so you can hear it . . . '

'A what-now?'

'A four-track recorder. It's what musicians use . . . '

'Man's from the streets, Herman. Man uses what man has.'

'Listen, Amit. I'm not trying to muscle in on your band or

anything. I just thought that, seeing as we both love rap, we could do some together.'

Silence. Deflection. Evasive manoeuvres. Coconut Unlimited did *not* need a white man in its ranks. It'd ruin the image big time.

'What you doing in my comic shop?'

'I've been listening to Wu Tang Clan and stuff, this tape that Ahmed made me, and they've got loads of heavy stuff on there and they're always rapping about comics and kung-fu so I thought I'd buy some comics, get some inspiration. Dad won't let me watch kung-fu. He says slitty eyes make him nervous.'

'Your dad needs to check himself before he wrecks himself.'

'Straight up racist. Whenever I'm bumping Biggie and Pac he's always banging on the door and shouting, "Turn that jungle bunny hop shit off now. Get it out of my house." I mean, what a racist . . . '

'Innit. He's never had any black friends.'

'No. Neither have I . . . can you introduce me to some? I need to check some lingo out with them, stuff I don't understand.'

'Like what? Man knows the lingo, seen? I can decipher for you.'

'Like, what's a strap? When they say stuff like "we come strapped" . . . what are they talking about?'

I paused.

'Being strapped is, like, having muscles . . . like, big muscles to pound your face with.'

I left the shop and started heading home, cutting out St George's to avoid any Ash dalliances.

I could hear them before I saw them. They were outside the off licence, giggling. Jasel and Pentil were clutching bottles of beer. Ahmed had a cigarette. They were all laughing hysterically. I put up the hood of my puffa and quickened my pace. It was either slip through this net or face St George's. They weren't as scary as Ash. We were out of school. Harrow was my endz.

Pentil looked up and squinted. Jasel turned and laughed uncontrollably. The theme music for *Black Beauty* erupted and they both started neighing. Jasel started the gallop towards me. I looked up and pulled my hood down.

'Come on, guys. We're not in school.' I had false swagger being in normal people clothes and knowing that, if I ran back the way I came, I could be protected by Ash in a second.

Jasel stopped mid-gallop. 'Bloody hell, Amit. When did you get so sensitive? It's just a joke.'

'You know we're all mates don't you? Really?' Pentil offered.

'Nah, *mate*. I ain't friends with racist pricks.'

'Racist?' Pentil stuttered. 'R–r–r–racist? What are you on about? I'm hanging with two Asians. How the hell does make me a racist? You idiot. I can't be racist if two of my friends are brown. Those are the rules.'

I looked at him. Jasel did too. Ahmed stubbed out the cigarette and shook his head.

'Whatever. I'm off home.'

'Nah, Amit, check it. You got to stay around for a second. Keep talking to us.'

'What? Why Jasel? Why do I want to talk to you?'

'Just . . . ' He trailed off as I saw it coming, a happening so crazy I thought I was hallucinating . . .

Behind Pentil's head, a car, a Polo, drove straight into the front of the off licence. I jumped in my self, in my skin, suddenly jolted like a hammer clanging a nail, like a spike on an EKG, like . . . a car driving into the front of a suburban off licence.

Ahmed and Jasel recoiled, while Pentil looked at the car then took off, running in the opposite direction as fast as he could, his beer bottle smashing on my big toe as I jumped back. Ahmed ran to the car, while the shop keeper and his employees were rooted to the spot, like marble wastemans.

Then I saw who was sitting in the front seat: Pete Hall, class stoner, holding the machete he concealed his drugs in, trying to cut himself out of his seatbelt, the steering wheel, nano-inches from the chin of his face, laughing to himself, laughing and crying in paroxysms. He freed himself, bashed against the car door till it opened and fell out, holding the machete aloft, the shop keeper standing over him with a 'what the what?' look plastered on his face. Pete was bellowing at him.

'I'll stab you if . . . your clothes, your boots, your motorcycle . . .' He laughed. 'No, hyeah, grrdsauurgle . . . bring me your cmcsif-fucking cigarettes . . . all of them. All of your Marlboro Lights and nothing else. Now! And a beer. I want a Stella. Now . . . or I'll tell them all you're a terrorist. Or I'll tell them you do kids . . . or I'll STAB YOU IN THE FACE.'

The shop keeper stood over Pete's flailing body, shocked, unable to move as Ahmed pushed him back. 'Call an ambulance!'

I was still, Jasel was too for a moment, before turning in the direction of Pentil – not that far, about 500 metres down the road, out of the strobe filters of culpability – and following him as nonchalantly as he could. Ahmed stared at him and shook his head. He turned to Pete who was banging against his shin with the machete, then fell on to him, knee first and choked him in the neck till he dropped the knife. He kicked it to one side and beckoned me over.

'If I roll him over, can you check if he's bleeding?'

'I . . . erm . . .'

'Pull yourself together, Amit. This is real! Man's hurt. Just check him for blood, blud.'

'I can't . . .'

Ahmed turned to the shop keeper. 'DID YOU CALL AN AMBULANCE?'

The shop keeper shrugged. 'I call son.'

'No, not your son. We need an ambulance.'

Pete was singing a Nirvana song. It sounded miserable, like suicide music. I was keeping my foot over the machete – the evidence – in case he went for it. Ahmed was calm and turned to the guy one more time.

'Seriously, you need to call an ambulance.'

151

'Man is drug, man . . . he is drug man. He can die.'

'Do you want him to die in front of your shop?'

'He die. I call son.'

'Forget your son!'

'Too late.' We turned around. It was Ash.

'You know this man?' he said, looking at me.

'Which one?'

'BOTH OF THEM PUSSYHOLE.'

'Yeah, erm, they go to my school . . . '

'So who destroyed my retirement plan shop window? I will destroy them in the face ya get me? YAGETME?'

'Man's stoned. What can we do?'

'Take care of your own. You?' He pointed to Ahmed. 'Are you Muslim?'

'What? What does that have to . . . '

'Fuck off!' Ash had pulled out his own machete and started towards Ahmed, jolting wildly.

'Right, why did this honky milk bottle motherfucker drive a car into my retirement plan shop window?'

'He's off his head,' I offered. 'Drugs . . . '

'Yeah, I can see that. I have a skull full of eyes. What happened?'

I was frozen, my hands in my pocket, an indignant hardman snarl on my face, clearing it quickly so Ash didn't think I had anything to do with this. I tried to slope off but was spotted.

'Oi, Mit, come here.'

I turned back. He had his foot on Pete's chest, a machete pointed at Ahmed and the real life version of my fake snarl on his face. Not to be trifled with. I looked at Ahmed, who shook his head at me and walked over nervously tripping on some shop debris. Pete was stroking the tip of Ash's gleaming white Nikes, staring upwards and laughing as he bumped his hips up and down on the floor.

'Wha gwarn Ash?' I asked, nervous, my heart pounding with the rhythm. I had finally mastered 4/4 beats in my head. Wrong time.

'Wha gwarn? Wha gwidarn? Wha gwoony? What are you talking about? Look at my dad's shop! You get me to provide your posh school with tings and they mash up my dad's shop. This never happened when I kept my circle close and my enemies closer. I will destroy you for this. '

'I had nothing to . . . I didn't . . . I . . . '

'You . . . can you stop stroking my foot you . . . wait . . . ' Ash was staring down at Pete. 'Wait, oh shit is that Pete? Pete what the hell man? Peter Piper Packed a Pick of Peppered Pickles, that you?'

Pete stopped giggling and stroking and ground-humping in recognition of his name. 'Hello Ash. That's some strong stuff you sold me this morning. I thought I was a bank robber. Did I get the swag?'

'Petey, bruv, what did you do?'

'I thought I was floating through time and then I had become the body of the great train robber, Reginald Diggs, and I had to rob a bank. But I had to get away from the cops first so I hot-wired a car and drove it to the bank and the bank vault is in the front of the bank so the only way to bank on banking the bank is to drive the car into the vault. Did we punch through the reinforced steel?'

Sirens pewtered in the background. It was time to leave. Ash had some hasty words with his dad, and I took this as my cue. Ahmed stalked off in the direction Jasel and Pentil had coward-astardly taken, but I was already on my long way round home. It was getting to the time when Mum would be asking questions. I quickened my pace.

'I'll walk you home,' Ash said, striding beside me.

'Erm, I have band practice . . . '

'Listen, little man, we're all good. I don't want this to interrupt our business strategy so I'll say this. You keep a low profile. This Pete thing ain't on you. It's on him and if it's on him then it's coming back my way. You weren't there, seen. You were just, you know, on your way to band practice with your boys, yeah? You want to hold on to my weed for me in case they come? The cops? In case they wanna know about me and my moneys? Yeah, you're a king, a don. I tell you what, I'll even look the other way if you wanna sample it here.' I felt a meaty hook hand burst into my puffa jacket pocket, touching up against my own hand, leaving a plastic wad of something in there. 'You're a king, Amit. You're a big dog now. Don't go selling any of that shit cos I know where you live. Get me?' He patted me on the back. 'I'll be round later for that shit. Seen?'

OhmyGod OhmyGod OhmyGod OhmyGod OhmyGod OhmyGod OhmyGod OhmyGod OhmyGod OhmyGod OhmyGod OhmyGod OhmyGod OhmyGod OhmyGod

Weed in my pocket. I could smell it. The earth sweet smell. Did it have to be lit to get me high? I could feel it caressing my eyes making me drowsy making me want to laugh, making me want to be apathetic about everything, making me addicted, making me want to do nothing else except smoke that shit.

OhmyGod OhmyGod OhmyGod OhmyGod OhmyGod OhmyGod OhmyGod OhmyGod OhmyGod OhmyGod OhmyGod OhmyGod OhmyGod OhmyGod OhmyGod

'NO,' I said to my brain, which repeated it to my eyeballs. 'I will *not* let you conquer me.'

I needed to stash this stuff. I needed to get home. I needed to get off the street just in case the cops knew/my parents knew/everyone knew.

I got home and ran up to my room, ignoring my mum's calls to dinner, physically pushing my sister out of my room, my heart panting like a mountain of mantras . . . *no*, there was no time for rhyming. I leaned against the closed door and pulled the package of illegal drugs out of my pocket. Illegal drugs in my hand. Illegal drugs in my mum and dad's house. Illegal. Against the law. This nasty stuff that ruined lives, turned people into idiots and broke up families in my hand.

It looked like mud and grass and twig, bundled up tightly into a plastic sandwich bag. I needed to find the best place to stash it. I pulled out my porn briefcase with the false bottom filled with magazines. No go – that'd be double incrimination. I looked in the built-in cupboard containing the boiler and a secret compartment above it that went into oblivion. There was nothing except a pipe and, hidden behind, a bag of 70s porno magazines I'd appropriated from the loft upstairs to mix things up a bit, but also for the weird fascination of seeing what girls looked like in the past and imagining if they still looked the same.

Behind the pipe would do. I grabbed a chair, climbed it and reached up into the hidden depths of the cupboard. There it could stay. Evil disgusting stuff. God, why did anyone smoke it? It made them look like complete idiots with their laughing and boringness and always needing to eat. What fools. I wondered why rappers smoked so much weed. You'd think living where they did, they needed to be on the edge all the time. They needed to keep their minds sharp so their guns didn't go off accidentally, or something. There was no relaxing time in the ghetto, no time to kick back when you were on the streets.

This was good stuff. Peril made me think vividly about the streets. I stored it up in my brain box for later lyrics.

I got down off the chair and closed the cupboard, opening it quickly again just to make sure you couldn't see the bag, even if you knew what you were looking for and searched in the exact spot you knew it was hiding.

Mum's call for dinner came again and I let her have this one. I ran down the stairs, kicking off my shoes and socks. (Dad hated people wearing shoes and socks in the house – he called them 'barbarians'.) At the bottom of the stairs, I wiped the film of panic off my forehead and went into the sweatbox kitchen where Mum, trying her once a week English dish so we didn't feel left out, had provided fish fingers, frozen chips and peas, all lovingly heated up in the oven. She smiled at me. I smiled back. She was in a good mood.

'How vas school?'

'Yeah, good thanks.'

'Good, good. I receiving a call today from your Latin teacher.'

'Oh right. Really?'

'Just to say how much he thinks you are good. Shame it is not science and maths and something useful but he says all your languages – In-ger-lish, French, German, Latin – are tip top notch.'

'Oh thanks Mum.'

'So . . . I saw Nishant's mum today.'

'Oh yeah?'

'She says you boys are doing a jig in a pub?'

'What?'

'You are performing a jig in a pub.'

Damn Nishant's mum and her niceness and openness and interest in her son's life, not to mention her subsequent ability to tell all about her son's movements warmly and comfortably.

'Yeah, that's right. It's an open mic. We thought we'd try it, just for relaxing.'

Playing the relaxing/studying hard comparison card was usually the way to get round Mum.

'Son, this music thing. Is this vhat you vant to do? Is it going to make you money, buy you nice house, make you comfortable? I just vant you to be happy. But can you be happy if you haven't got songs to make money?'

'Mum, rappers make loads of money. They live in big houses in LA with swimming pools and granny flats and everything.'

The granny flat was also a good card to play on Mum. Whenever she wanted to make Nish and me feel really guilty about not studying hard enough, she questioned whether we'd be able to provide for our dear mum in her old age, as was the custom of our ancestors. Who would she live with? Could we afford houses with enough room for her? It was her biggest worry.

'I cannot stop you doing jig. I know Nishant's mum is going so she vill be superwising. I am not happy but I vill let you do this vone. If you promise that the band vill stop till summer holiday aftervards. You have GCSE mocks. If you do not pass, vhat happens?'

'Nothing. That's why they're called "mocks" . . . '

'I don't think this music is right. But you are right, this is leisure time, I cannot interfere. If you come home drunk and vith drugs I vill be heartbroken about my firstborn son who cannot take care of his own mother because he took the drugs and got addicted and spent all his money on it and lost his job, vhich vas only in factory.'

'Mum . . . Dad worked in a factory.'

'He vorked in factory so you don't have to!'

'Will you come to the gig?'

'No. Vhen do I have time for jigs? Vith your sister and your dad and you, it's like I hawe three children. I vork sewen days a veek. Vhen can I come to jig? Vhen I am rich housevife like Nishant's mum, then I come to jig.'

I needed to disengage her from this conversation. I sat down and did the stoic silence thing while she went off on a tangent about my lack of focus, usually paraphrasing from conversations with Dad, using his soundbites, slightly wrong. I ate my three fish fingers and handful of blackened chips, and saved my peas for last. I went to grab a Coke from the fridge to wash it down.

'Coke? At this time of day? Vhy don't you drink something good for you?' Mum heckled from the rotis she was rolling for tomorrow, almost autistically needing to re-fill the kitchen with Indian food smells after tainting it with western frozen rubbish. 'Dhud pi [drink milk] pani pi [drink water].'

I slammed the fridge shut and left the kitchen, running up the stairs and into Dad, who was inhaling deeply.

'There is a strange smell in this upstairs part of the house,' he said, flaring his nostrils and drawing in a big nose-breath.

'What's that Dad?' Oh my God was he, like, a sniffer dog?

'Something smells sweet. It is strange. Vhat is it?'

'Dunno, Dad . . . '

He grabbed my arm and pulled me close, clutching my mouth under his nose. 'Have you been smoking?'

'NO DAD.'

'Good boy.' That was his weird weekly smoking check. He was convinced I'd sully my body with that rubbish. But it wasn't over. He followed me into my room, sniffing. 'Strange smell,' he assured me, peeking into my room. 'Are the vindows closed?'

'Yes, why?'

He looked at me suspiciously. 'Vhy you ask me, your father, a question?'

He stared into my eyes. Then I smelt it. That weird earthy sweet smell. Floating. Just a tinge. A twinge. A little minge of aroma wafting out of my room. I looked at him and shrugged. I didn't know what the problem was. I needed to disengage. I needed everyone to leave me alone to think my way out of this conversation.

'Anyways, Dad, I got homework to do . . . '

'Vhy are you paranoid?'

He pulled me closer to him, via my chin, peering into my eyes, then let go.

'I'm not paranoid, Dad, just busy . . . GCSE coursework and that . . . '

He looked at me, grimaced and bounded down the stairs, holding on to the sides of the walls for steadying, stumbling slightly. He was five glasses of booze down, the hound.

I got back in my room, ignoring Mum's screams and yelps for help clearing up. The door closed, the chair back in place, the hand puncturing the air behind the pipe, the sear and burn the hot hot heating always on all year round for my permanently cold mother, the weed, trapped underneath, not melting but the plastic hot, releasing some perfume into the air.

I pulled the weed out and stared at it, the plastic wet with heat.

I needed to get this stuff out of my house, and fast. I put it in my pocket, pulled the chair away and closed the cupboard door. Looking around the room for something that wasn't heat or cold-conducting, I fixated on the briefcase – the porn case with the false bottom. That's where it needed to go. I pulled the briefcase from under the bed, resting underneath some vinyl sleeves I'd taken from our stash for perusing. I liked looking at the covers. There was an aura of mystique, like I was channelling a higher spirit simply by having the sleeves in my house. The part of the band the others would never get, this was the burden of being the principal songwriter.

The briefcase was open, the false bottom quivering with boobs and big red hair – a favourite of mine at the time – the weight of the worth-something comics concealing the panel. I pulled up the comics then thought better of it and slid the weed into one of the trays in the lid. The worst thing in the world would be trying to sell these comics in thirty years and people finding traces of weed, devaluing them. That would not be good for sales, or my pension plan.

The tray filled with my illegal stash, the briefcase closed, the vinyl weights returned to the top, the push under the bed and I was less panicked. Mum wouldn't dream of going through that case. She knew it contained my nest egg comics, and she knew opening the case could adversely effect her potential granny flat prospects. The lengths I had to go to, for any semblance of privacy.

With the briefcase safely stored, I decided to heed my Mum's calls for help clearing up after dinner, to stock up on karma. I strolled downstairs like the coolest kitty cat in the litter tray and nodded at her.

'What's up?'

'Nothing is up. Vhy is something always up? Does something have to be up?'

'No, Mum. Sorry . . . erm . . . ' I trailed off. 'Play it cool man,' I thought. 'You don't need any further probing into your life.'

'I mean, who vould say to their mother vhat is up like something is up and I'm up and you're down and everybody is cool, *man*. Nothing is up. You are speaking less like a gora and more like a kala. Always oondho. Such oondho.'

I sat down at the table as Dad burst in. 'Come here,' he said, grabbing me.

I was apoplectic with hectic worry. I was manic with panic. I was done for.

I was going to be arrested for the sale and distribution of class A DRUGS and I was going to die in prison. Unless Dad wrote this off as a lapse of judgement and didn't shop me to the cops.

No chance. He was a stickler for the rules. Once, my mum had come home from the supermarket and admitted she'd forgotten to pay for a box of French Fancies she'd accidentally left in the trolley. She was considering donating it to the homeless guy outside Harrow station, or throwing it away because of the guilt. She couldn't eat and enjoy the cakes. Dad threatened to phone the police and drove her back to the supermarket, explaining the whole thing to the confused shop manager, who just told him to forget about it and leave with the box. Dad refused, said it was wrong and left the box for him to deal with. He stormed through the shop to the cakes and treats aisle, picked up a new box and paid for it, pushing it into my mum's crumbling embarrassed fingers and driving her home, fuming. There was no way he was letting me walk away from this.

Except, he didn't take me upstairs to my briefcase. Instead, he led me into the lounge where the TV was blasting the news.

On the screen was the local news, explaining that a fourteen-year-old boy high on LSD, weed and cocaine, who went to my school, had driven his car into an off-licence near Harrow.

[We are getting reports that Pete Hall is the son of local police chief . . .]
[The private school that Pete Hall goes to is also the same

160

as where Pat Sharpe, presenter of TV's *Fun House* sends
his children . . .]
[The fees alone make this one of the most exclusive
schools in the area . . .]
[The local Gujarati community were not happy with the
demolition of their local community cash and carry . . .]
['Vhere vill vee buy our alkool now?]

'This is your classmate?'

'Yes.'

'You know him?'

'Yes . . . but we're not friends. He's a bit weird . . . '

'Look vhat he did. Is this vhat you're doing vhen you are doing
the jigs vith Anand and Nishant?'

'No, Dad.'

'Well, I do not know vhat to think. There is drugs at my son's
school. There is violence at my son's school. Vhat do I pay those
fees for?'

'And vhy do vee vork sewen days a veek, killing ourselwes for this
to happen?' Mum added, like an automaton, hearing key phrases.

Dad looked at me. 'I hope you are not inwolwed vith this.'

'No, Dad.'

I trundled back into the kitchen, in shock. Holy majoly Pete
made the evening news with that stupid shenanigan. Maybe that's
why I hadn't heard from Ash about collecting his weed. Every time
the phone rang, though, I tensed up in case it was him, or Pentil
and Jasel wanting to collaborate on stories. My head was a mess,
and I couldn't help but descend into big baller rhymes . . .

> *This shit is all messed up, I'm outta luck*
> *Played with fire, feel really tired, in loads of muck*
> *Cos of Ash, this local dealer he got me getting connects*
> *If I don't he's threatened me with bad bum sex*
> *I'm vex cos now the band hasn't practised for days*
> *Been ducking out cos of all these boys and their straight hate*

I'm late for the date cos my mates don't relate to my fate
I'm at the gate, I'm turning straight, I'm losing weight
My mum and dad want to know why I know all these people
My best friends want to know why I keep them up the steeple

*   *   *

Nishant was upset when I recounted the story the next day. He was desperate to keep Ash out of our lives and failing. He could see me slipping deeper, could spy the despair in my eyes as we walked to school. He'd tried to call me all evening but the phone was engaged, due to my sister and her gossip network. He told us that everything was changing and he'd only just managed, thanks to the band, to now accept us as a three rather than a duo and me as an add-on.

Anand told me that the story had made the *Daily Mail*. I was shocked. It'd made the papers? How long before they poked around and found out about my involvement? The story talked about what had happened and how Pete's dad was a policeman, and our entire school was all on drugs. I stopped walking. The school gates were looming.

'I'm in trouble,' I said.

I didn't know if I should let them know about the stash I was holding for Ash, but I needed to tell someone. It'd been twelve hours and he hadn't come to collect. I needed it out of my house.

'Did it mention any names?' I snapped back into focus.

'What?' Anand had moved on to describing the costume he was going to wear at next week's open mic, which was looming.

'Did the bloody article mention any names?' I implored.

'Nah, they can't do that. We're minors so it's a minor ting man. Relax. You don't smoke anything and they can test that shit . . . '

What if they tested my room, though? And the pocket of my jeans from yesterday? I needed to get them in the wash quicksmart, my new natty jeans. Only problem was, Mum had faded them on the first wash and I didn't want them to fade even more.

'Anand, what about fibres?'

'What?'

'Did the article mention anything about clothing fibres?'

'What's wrong with you? It's like you paranoid from smoking or something.' Some kids from the year below walked past, eyeballing me after Anand's comment.

'Listen man, I'm pure. I got nothing to worry about.'

With false bravado, it was time to go into those school gates and get ourselves a low profile. Time to show them I had nothing to worry about.

But then I saw Pentil and Jasel waiting at the end of the path, by the school gates, looking at me. The long path.

I listened to Anand go on about this new denim suit he'd procured from somewhere, and Nishant tell us about finding different items for his outfit from a charity shop. They assumed I was having one of my quiet thinking moments, plotting and planning for the future of the band.

Jasel and Pentil were blatantly waiting for me. They wanted to collude and mix up stories and get our plan together. I wondered if Ash had talked to them, if he'd seen the article and realised his big operation was about to get exposed. Then I wondered if he even read newspapers.

Anand and Nishant stood in a triangle in front of me as we approached Pentil and Jasel. They were shifting nervously. I kept my head down, imagining a hoodie protecting my head.

'Yo Nishant, Anand . . . ' Jasel approached them, his hand outstretched. 'Get lost, yeah. We need to speak to your man . . . '

'I'm staying with my friend and put your hand in your pocket or I'll judo chop it off,' Nishant said, adopting a Shaolin stance. 'I saw them do it in a film. I'm sure I can do it too . . . '

'We don't want trouble,' Pentil said, smiling at me. 'We just want to chat to Amit.'

'These are my friends. You want something from me? You ask me in front of my friends. We ain't got secrets.'

'OK, look. What you gonna say about the weed?'

'What weed?' I said, wondering if they knew about Ash's stash.

'The weed that Ash sold us.'

'Ain't shizz to do with me. I just want a quiet life, bruv. Laters . . . ' I started to walk away.

'Look Amit,' said Pentil, blocking me, 'they're gonna ask you . . . '

'Why?'

'Cos the teachers know you know Ash.'

'How's that?'

Jasel was contrite, sheepish. He said he'd told them I was there when the car crashed into the shop.

'And the cops know we were all there too,' Pentil added.

'I'm gonna have to talk to the police? Look, just leave me alone, yeah?'

'Yeah, let him go!' Nishant shook his fist.

I started to walk away but, just like in a film where they wait for someone to walk away before delivering the crunch information, so they can do the shocked look-backwards thing, Jasel said, 'You don't know do you?'

I looked back, and stopped. 'Know what?'

'Ash's been arrested. The car knocked over a hollow part of the wall in the shop where he keeps his gear. He's locked up.'

'So?'

'So?' said Pentil, worked up. 'So? You introduced us to him and he's in prison now. We might all end up there.'

'I didn't do anything. I introduced one man, against my will I might add, to another. What's any of this got to do with me?'

'Because they want to know how all the drugs are getting into the school,' said Jasel.

'Yeah, and . . . ?'

'And . . . we want your assurance that they aren't coming through us.'

'I don't know and I don't care.'

'Look Amit,' Pentil said. 'I'll be square with you. If you tell them we're dealing drugs in school, we'll tell them you're dealing drugs in school . . . '

I could see him trying not to falter. It was only two per cent comforting to know he was as nervous as me.

I pushed past, grimacing at not being stronger than him, and patted my only two friends in school on the back before letting them lead me inside.

On the way to my classroom, Anand told me about Meena and how she'd let him put a straw in her vagina and blow in. He then showed us this new kissing technique he'd picked up called 'washing machine', which involved swirling your tongue around thoroughly like a washing machine chugging to a halt after a vicious spin cycle. For two minutes, I forgot everything else going on and listened to him describe how black Meena's nipples were. I didn't care anymore if he was just bullshitting and manning, or if he was actually bamming her.

I nodded at my boys and pushed into my classroom, feeling the silence blam then lick then kick me in the face. Everyone was looking at me. BS was standing with his arms on his hips, staring at the door.

'Chuckles,' he said somberly. 'Come with me. The rest of you, shut up. This is not the day for it.'

'Is there a problem, Sir?' I asked, nervous.

'Just come with me,' he said. Gone the bluster, gone the rail roading, gone the attempts at humour, gone the race-tinged insults. This was serious.

On the way out we walked into Pentil and Jasel, hurrying in, red-faced. I looked back at them as BS led me away. Jasel threw his fist up in a black power salute, like we were in this together. Pentil stared at the ground.

'Chuckles.'

'Yes, Sir?'

'You are to report to the headmaster's office. Go straight there.

Do not deviate from this course. Do you understand the words coming out of my mouth?'

'Yes, Sir.'

'Good. Go. Now.'

He spirited off back to the classroom and I trundled up the corridor, panicking. I had to keep reminding myself, 'You haven't done anything you gimp. Why are you so afraid? Guilt by association?' I'd courted the bad men and now I was about to pay for it.

I freestyled myself along.

> *I done it – I done the crime, I do the time*
> *I'm dangerous, I bathe in grime*
> *Tell your mum I'm trying to do better*
> *But I can't help making bodies wetter*
> *With blood, that's what you get when you cross me*
> *One day I'll be away away behind lock and key*
> *Look at me now full of regret*
> *Wishing that one day I'll give what I get*
> *And not take what I give*
> *And get what I take in order to live*
> *I'll shiv you in prison, my head shaped like a prism*
> *I see you shooting jissom on your porn filums . . .*

'Chuckles!'

Why was I so good at freestyling in my head where no one could hear my genius?

I turned round. BS was standing in the doorway of his classroom, hands on hips.

'Hurry. Now. Go. Now.'

'Yes, Sir.'

I turned back in the direction of my doom. The rhymes had me fired up. Existential. Taking responsibility for my actions. Yeah you posh wankers, I did the crime, I'll do the time. Ya get me. I'm Mit Dogg, bitches, all AKs blazing with the taste of bass for your face. I got the gunz, I got the planz . . .

'CHUCKLES!'

BS was still waiting for me to hurry up. I ran off in the direction of the headmaster's office, pursing my brain with questions.

Will I be expelled?

Will being expelled be good promo for the band?

What are Mum and Dad going to say?

Why don't I just run off now and live on the streets, get a drugs connect and start slinging?

What time is the open mic?

Do we arrive late or early?

Why me?

I imagined the beat dropping as I whispered, 'Why me?' The headnodding beat with muted but funky drums rolling and swinging on the one and the two and the three and the four, Mit Doggy Dogg coming through your big white door. Yo. The stabs of trumpets, full of soul but sombre too, full of life but depressed as well, full of dancing hips but with the struggle of slavery ships too. The bass rolling and throbbing like a heartbeat, like you're dancing but you've got sad eyes, like you're giving it all in your headnod because what else is there in your life? This was my soundtrack for the walk to Roseblade's office. This was the movement that propelled me forwards like . . .

Baow . . . Ba–baooooow

Ba–boom–boom–ba ba–boom–boom–ba baba–boom–boom–ba baba–boom–boom–ba.

Baow . . . Ba–baooooow

Ba–boom–boom–ba ba–boom–boom–ba baba–boom–boom–ba baba–boom–boom–ba.

Baow . . . Ba–baooooow

Ba–boom–boom–ba ba–boom–boom–ba baba–boom–boom–ba baba–boom–boom–ba.

Baow . . . Ba–baooooow [daka–daka–dum–dum–dum–da–da–dum–dum–da–da–da–da]

Ba–boom–boom–ba ba–boom–boom–ba baba–boom–boom–ba baba–boom–boom–ba.

Baow . . . Ba–baooooow [daka–daka–dum–dum–dum–da–da–dum–dum–da–da–da–da]

I stand accused of being a man who done the plan stole your grand
I stand accused of being the man who had the gunz and the funds
I stand alone and I moan about the phone not ringing
No one's bringing me the work to jerk me to where I lurk
I stand here . . . I stand with no fear . . . I don't beer
I shed no tears . . .

At the end of the corridor was a branch out to the right, a wing where the offices of the school hierarchy and the school secretary were. I stood at the end.

'I'm a man,' I thought to myself. 'I'm ready. Take me away to Riker's Island. Bigger men than me have fallen there and I'm ready, ya get me? I'm ready . . . '

The door opened and Mr Roseblade appeared, all five-foot-five of him, standing shoeless, his greying blonde spiky hair standing to attention. I walked towards him and he pointed at my feet. I pulled my shoes off toe-heel, as required by law in this sanctum, and entered.

The office was bigger than two classrooms. It had a desk overlooking the field, sprayed with white reams of paper, all with his tiny red pen annotations. Every wall had wall-to-wall bookcases, filled with books and books, most of them with the classic hardback slightly goldy spine. There was a daybed with a sleeping bag stashed conspicuously underneath it and a seating area around a television and video player, and another around a coffee table. It was this he ushered me towards. He pointed to a fizzing glass of Coke and biscuits and ushered me to take them.

No, I mentally decided. I want nothing from you.

I waited for him to invite me to sit. He didn't. He sat, laughing to himself maniacally. He hadn't spoken. He–he–he, kinda like a machine gun guffaw . . . heeheehee.

'Sit down, Amit,' he finally said, pointing to a seat.

He looked at me and, gradually, the Joker smile poured inwards to create a stern expression. He looked at my glass of Coke and placed his hand on his chin, resting his head on his knuckles.

'Yes, OK, well. Read the papers today?'

'Yes, Sir.'

'Do you think the type of school I want to run is one that allows people to take illegal drugs?'

'No, Sir.'

'Good. Now tell me, what kind of school do you want to go to?'

'Sir, a good school, where I can do my work.'

'Interesting. Yes. A good school. And what makes a good school?'

'Students who behave?'

'Wow. Just wow. Wow, amazing. Wow. You got it. Students who behave, and behave they must. Let me tell you a story about Woody Allen and then you'll see where I'm coming from. Woody Allen is from New York and he's Jewish and he's very funny, you see. He made films about his relationships and *Annie Hall* was actually about Diane Keaton the actress in the film because Diane is Diannie and Diannie is Annie and can you guess what her maiden name was? No? Try, it's fairly obvious from the direction this story is heading. She was Diane Hall before she got married, making her . . . yes, you guessed it, Annie Hall. And see, in the opening of the film, he does this monologue. *There's an old joke – um . . . two elderly women are at a Catskill mountain resort, and one of 'em says, "Boy, the food at this place is really terrible." The other one says, "Yeah, I know; and such small portions." Well, that's essentially how I feel about life – full of loneliness, and misery, and suffering, and unhappiness, and it's all over much too quickly.* Do you see what I'm saying?'

A pause.

'That's the problem with teenagers,' he continued, when I didn't say anything. 'You can't read between the lines. Only what's in front of you. I'm trying to say, DON'T BRING DRUGS INTO MY SCHOOL EVER AGAIN. OR YOU WILL FEEL

THE LONELINESS AND MISERY AND SUFFERING AND UNHAPPINESS OF EXPULSION.' He was standing, booming. I was recoiling.

'Sir, erm, not all black people are drug dealers. I'm clean. I've not done anything . . . '

'Clean. Black. Hmm, yes. OK, first rebuttal would be questioning whether you're black. Hmm, was your father from Africa?'

'Kenya, Sir.'

'Yes, I suppose that does make you black. Well, OK, let's see. Am I accusing you of dealing drugs in my school because you're black? Actually, what are you? In terms of social demographics?'

'I'm a British-born third generation Indian with a Kenyan father and a Yemenese mother. But I grew up in Harrow. I'm a Harrow boy . . . '

'Etymology is fascinating. It reminds me of the film *Predator*. How the hunter can become the hunted. How we're all predators. Fascinating stuff. OK, fine. So you claim to not be a drug dealer because you're black. Is that right?'

'Yes, Sir.'

'OK, that's fascinating. I mean, I think I really need to look at my motivations in accusing you. But first, we need to talk about the drug dealing. Because if you're just pulling the race card all I'm going to say is this: make it stop now. OK? I have fees to think about and low level street dealing in my halls and corridors is something I cannot and will not abide. OK?'

Did I confirm or did I continue to deny? I denied. 'Sir but it's not me!'

'I'm talking in hypotheticals. Work with me.'

'Sorry, Sir . . . '

He paused. I looked around the room at the paintings of the other headmasters, all sterner sorts than him. His painting, already up despite him still being in post, showed his shit-eating grin to the fullest. I stared up at it and scanned down to his perplexed face now, in this room. I noted the placing of the portrait, across from his desk. Maybe it was so he could look up at it and cheer himself up.

'OK, Chuckles.' He broke the silence with *that* name. 'New tack here, we're going to try this instead. You tell me who is dealing drugs in my school and I tell you you can leave and no more is spoken of this. Have you heard of McCarthy? I want you to name names, Chuckles. Name names. Go on, name names. Name me some names.'

'Names of what?'

'You are an infuriating British-born Harrow-bred third generation Indian with a Kenyan father and a Yemenese mother. You know what I mean. Name the names of the street level dealers who are supplying drugs in my school from your friend, Ash, currently a guest of Her Majesty's finest borstal.'

So Ash *is* in jail? What the what? What about his weed? How long was he away for? Did I need to hold it for him?

'I don't know, Sir. I don't hang out with anyone except Anand and Nishant. They're my only friends here.'

'How strange. Why not?'

'Sir, I'm not a drug dealer.'

'Name names.'

'I don't know any names.'

'OK, look, we'll try it this way. You can . . . erm . . . you can . . . ' He sat back in his chair and smiled at me. Then he placed his hands behind his head and rubbed at the gnawing scalp peeking through a whisp of his spiky but decaying blonde hair. 'Speculate. You have to speculate to accumulate. So speculate. Who do you think it is?'

'I don't know,' I said, looking away.

He leaned forwards, the darkness implanted in his face again.

'Look, you little *wog*,' he hissed. 'I have a meeting with the governors and I need to assure them this is going to go away. I have an interview with the *Daily Mail* and I need to make it go away.'

'Sir, I think you know the types of people who'd be doing what you're talking about. And you know I'm not one of them. And know this: I ain't no snitch. Snitches is for bitches.'

I smiled inwardly at my rap reference. Nice.

Then I looked at his dark-mooded face fluctuate between angry and smoothed-over-smile. He couldn't decide. His eyebrows sank towards each other and he leaned forwards again. Roseblade was lost for words.

He stood up and pointed me to the door. As I stood up and started to leave the room, I peered back at the painting of Curtis, the headmaster fired for beating children and kicking them in the arse, at the photo of Mellor, the whisp-gentle giant who'd spent my interview for the school asking me to translate sentences into Gujarati for my parents. I was eleven. I saw the older head-masters, growing in sternness as time threw them backwards into the lineage of past authority figures. Roseblade led me towards the door. His hand hovered for comfort near my shoulder in case I needed it. I was shaking with fear and anger – fear that I'd get into trouble for this at home, and anger that I was here instead of Pentil.

Roseblade opened the door to usher me out. Outside in the corridor, Nishant and Anand were standing with their heads bowed and fists pumped in the Black Panther salute, their ties undone and turned to the black side, tied round their biceps in support of my cause.

Nishant looked up as the door opened. 'Free the Asian One!'

'Get back to class, you idiots!'

Anand held his stance. Nishant did a twirl and held out his Black Panther hand as if to say, 'Stop! HAMMER TIME.'

'Free the Asian One!'

Mrs Hamster, the school secretary, ran out and put her hands to her cheeks in overly-dramatic fashion. 'Sir, they barged past . . . '

'Sir,' Nishant interrupted, 'we are not drug dealers, we are not thieves and killers, we are not dangerous. We are people too. We are humans. FREE THE ASIAN ONE.'

'He's free to go.'

'Good. I don't have to pull out my evidence files then.'

Nishant twirled and led me off. Anand looked up, eyeballed Roseblade and followed.

'And your ties go on your collar . . . NOW!' Roseblade screamed after us down the corridor.

I was shaking, I was flaking, I was baking – I was taken with nerves. I turned as a burst of bile brimmed up through my body, and birthed itself on to the floor with a satisfying slap.

Next: Give me the microphone before I buss up my pants

CHAPTER SEVEN

Protec Ya Neck

Live and direct. We were gonna bring it, live and direct.

Mum was asleep in the car outside, waiting till after our slot. She insisted on picking me up and dropping me due to the nature of the venue. I had to request an early slot or she'd make good on her threat to come and get me and take me home. Nishant's mum was there too, but to support. I milled near the car as she invited Mum to come into the pub with her and watch us perform. Mum refused, saying she'd been working all day and didn't have the energy. What she didn't say was that we'd had an argument when I went to leave for the gig, and she went effing nuts.

'Vhere are you going?'

'Just out, Mum, to see Anand and Nishant.'

'Whose houvse?'

'Erm . . . Nishant's.'

'Vell, I vant her to drop you home. I don't vant drunk school-boys to crash into you with their cars-bars.' She thrust her oscillating head in a violent jerk left. She didn't look up from the chapati she was rolling, her small right foot, coloured pink to hide the gnarled long toenails, clamped onto the kitchen bench.

'I'll be fine.'

'Look, I am tired. I have been vorking all veek and I vant you to listen to your mother. Nobody in this country listens to their mother.'

'I'll be back early.'

'I vill phone Naina. She vill understand about vanting to protect her son.'

'Mum . . .'

She reached for the portable phone and switched it on, leaning back so she could see the numbers.

'Mum . . . '

Then I told her where I was going. I told her about the gig. I told her about the band. I told her how important the open mic was. She'd banned me from going in the morning, even though yesterday we were all good, an acquiesence to get me to work. I was going anyway. I told her so. I told her about Nishant's dancing. I was so weary, sick of keeping secrets, sick of knowing too much. Sick of the burdens. Sick and tired.

She went mental. Absolutely mental. She got so upset she started crying and complaining about how I was destroying every dream she and my dad had for me, about going to university and getting a decent job, about making the most of my education, about the melange of possibility I was throwing away just by indulging in stupidness that had nothing to do with studying. She threw her rolling pin against the floor.

I pleaded with her. I told her I had to go. I told her about the music scouts that came to the Fat Controller open mic to spot new talent. I didn't tell her that I didn't know if music scouts came to the Fat Controller open mic to spot new talent or not. It was a conservative guess based on the assumption that the Fat Controller open mic was one of the few in a circuit I had no knowledge of, so it stood to reason it'd be a hotbed of un-discovered talents and entrepreneurial spirits wishing to exploit them.

Mum relented, but insisted on coming with me. She turned the dhal off, stopped rolling chapatis, told Dad that dinner (read: leftovers) was in the fridge and said she'd wait in the car. She also said she'd smell my breath at the end of the gig, and when she heard Auntie Naina was coming she was happy to have a spy, a fellow traveller in the war on drugs in my school. She was a *Daily Mail* reader, after all.

This was a curious habit that I never quite understood. They'd pour over that newspaper every day over breakfast, usually Indian gathia and hot chai, and reel off statistics about immigrants and how awful they were.

'These bloody Bengalis are all same,' Dad would say. 'Coming here, colonising our city and making it smell like dried fish. Disgusting Muslim immigrants.'

Irony or not, immigrant-haters they were. They hated the blacks, the Eastern Europeans, the Chinese, Japanese, loud Australians, dirty Bengalis, barbaric Pakistanis and stupid Sri Lankans. They hated Africans and Caribbeans. They hated South Americans and South Africans. They weren't even all that keen on white English, people they labelled as lazy, ignorant, stupid and backwards, who didn't care about their families. Yet my mum and dad were here, proudly siding with those they labelled as lazy and ignorant and stupid and backwards and not caring about their families, because they *were* a power structure of note, against everyone else. It was a cycle of useless prejudice.

Mum and Dad read the *Daily Mail* exposé and demanded to know why I hadn't told them about it. They wanted to know exactly what I knew about drug-taking. They were shocked that rich people did drugs. They were surprised that it existed in school at all. Dad had phoned up to speak to Roseblade, who had suddenly become indisposed.

I'd disposed of Ash's stash by now, thanks to Nishant. After my face-to-face with Roseblade, we left school together. Anand had excused himself to go and break up with Meena for the fourth time. Nishant bought me a can of Fanta and we sat behind Harrow-on-the-Hill train station, on the patch of grass where the sixth formers of the local college sat, and I broke down and told him the whole story. About Ash. About Jasel and Pentil. About the drugs in my cupboard. He'd been understanding, till we got to the drugs bit. He became serious and told me how we were going to get out of this pickle. Nishant was a crisis-manager.

'First thing we need to do, Amit, is realise we do not need to fear Ash anymore. He's in jail, locked up. He can't touch you anymore. So what I want you to do is close your eyes, and imagine a big red bin. This is the bin of your fears. Now pick up the lid. Hold it in your right hand. You're a leftie aren't you? OK, now imagine you're pulling all your fear of Ash out of your brain and placing it into the bin. Pull the fear out, and put it in the bin. Now, put the lid back on and open your eyes. How do you feel?'

'Better, thanks.'

I didn't feel better. I felt the same. Except I was mildly irritated having wasted a precious minute of my life. But I had to go along with it. He was only trying to help.

'OK, now we don't fear Ash. I'll be practical Amit. Ash is in jail. He doesn't want that weed anymore. He isn't gonna get out and come bashing down your door demanding it. He's going to want you to get rid of it because it's weed, it'll have his fingerprints too. You both want to get rid of it, OK? We can do it by . . .'

'Selling it?' I offered.

'Burning it.'

'What if we get high off the fumes?'

'Weed doesn't work like that. It only works if it's in the paper cos of chemical reactions.'

'Where do we burn it?'

'We put it in one of those metal bins, pour in some vegetable oil and a match. POOF! And it's gone. Out of our lives forever. And we go and win that open mic.'

'OK,' I sniffled.

Some Asian idiots, all in shaved heads with sculpted eyebrows, Tupac T-shirts and black baggy jeans with orange Tims, were gathered nearby blowing kisses at us, as if Nishant was breaking up with me and I was crying or something.

'Ignore them,' he said. 'We got some weed smoking to do.'

Getting it out of the house proved more difficult than I imagined, given that Nish was on a mammoth conversation with Rachna about Mr Nutter, their maths teacher, and what a git he was, while Mum was utilising Nishant's height to do some reaching for her. She kept him in the kitchen making small talk, despite calling him a 'bevakoof'.

I was anxious. I pulled the phone out of the socket and my sister out of my room. I was desperate. She screamed and barged back into my room. I lifted her up, immediately dropping her when I realised what I was doing.

'Please Nish. Give me ten minutes then you can use my room for the rest of the night. I won't stop you.'

'Whatever, Coco. And I'm telling Dad you hit me.' She left my room.

'NISHANT!' I yelled, at the top of my voice. I heard him bounding up the stairs, my mum calling after him. He pulled into my room and slammed the door shut.

I grabbed my briefcase from under the bed, unpacked it and pulled the cellophane of plant out.

'I don't want it,' he said, shaking his head then taking it out of my hand, curiously inspecting the package. 'Come on,' he urged.

He shoved the weed back at me and I pushed it deep into my pocket. I replaced the chair and we bounded back down the stairs, out the house into the suburban pacifier of the Harrow suburbs. I looked up at the drizzle sky. Nishant opened his coat a little and showed me the small bottle of vegetable oil and matches he'd stolen from Mum. I pulled him away because she was looking at him through the kitchen window, and we headed to the park.

Nishant had a plan. We wound through Harrow's residential streets, lined with masis and bas, floral sarees flapping in the wind, dipping from foot to foot, ambling slowly along. The edge of the park was in sight. He led me, quickly and silently, towards the always-empty public loos – always empty because of the stench of urine, gang graffiti on the doors and the fact that there was never any toilet paper. We entered. It was a hive of smells, putrid, so thick you could taste it at the back of your tongue. The shit hanging heavy in the air, reminding me of India when I was six, Nishant of growing up in Mombasa, care-free, with an outhouse for kaka-business.

We stood next to a bowl. Nishant pulled out the cooking oil and matches and kicked a bin, teeming with tissue, into the centre of the room. I closed the door on his instruction, begrudging the smell we were trapped with. He upended the cooking oil into the bin and pulled out a match, lit it and dropped it in. Flames burst up, quickly, streaming like a water fountain of fire towards the ceiling, where a sprinkler burst and some drizzle half-hearted its way into the room.

'Quick then!' he urged. I pulled out the weed and he grabbed it, throwing it into the bin. He lit another match for good measure, the flames subsisting to the sprinkler drizzle. The weed burned.

'Do you think it'll burn my fingerprints off?' I said.

'It should do.'

'I just worry about DNA and evidence and stuff.'

'Me too. But hey, it's OK. It's done. Look . . . '

We peered in. The weed was on fire, flaming orange, that smell pulsing around the room.

We looked at each other, sniffing.

'We can't get high off this can we?' I said.

Nishant giggled, stifled it and added, 'I don't think so. Doesn't it need paper to mix with?'

'Are you sure?' I said. 'It's just, I definitely feel weird. And hungry. And that's a symptom of being high isn't it?'

'Yeah,' he said, looking worried.

'Should we leave?'

'We can't. We started a fire. It could get out of control. We could burn the building down.' Nishant was the fire safety marshall at school. Never off duty.

'Nishant . . . I feel high. I feel stoned. I want to laugh but I'm stopping myself.'

'Me too.'

'I'm scared. I might go and sit in one of the toilets.'

He stayed by the fire to make sure it was burning, breathing in the earthy sweet aroma of boom kali weed. I headed to a cubicle, to another and another, finding them all unflushed and seat-less with a thick stream of piss to wade through. This whole place was covered in DNA, I realised, feeling relieved.

I turned to Nishant, stifling a grin.

'Free-style,' he said, and laughed.

I stood there, hearing the beat in my head.

> *Words and ideas are my weapons of choice*
> *My voice is louder than the gunfire and the street noise*
> *All I need is a pen and pad, the tools of my trade*
> *Spit my justice at the soul blockades*
> *Cascades of truth in my mind's insurrection*
> *Slowly and surely we will find the right direction*
> *I will keep on fighting till all walls falls*
> *Knock 'em down to the ground with a wreckin' ball . . .*

Nishant, his eyes watering with the intense mix of fire smoke and weed smoke, applauded me, smiling. I nodded, amazed at how good I sounded. Maybe this was what pressure did to a man. Maybe I just needed to be more on edge to help bring out my safe lyricals.

> *When you see me do you really wanna be me?*
> *Do I epitomise what an Asian should be?*
> *Whatever the case, when you see my face,*
> *I bet the first thing you think of is my race*
> *Maybe I'm a troublemaker from the slum*
> *That'll rob your mum, the kinda scum that has no income*
> *Looking like I've succumbed to hard drugs and the cops*
> *Or maybe I just earn ten cornershops*

'Wooohooo!' Nishant whooped. 'You're on fire!'

'No . . . ' I said, 'but that weed is.'

We both turned to the smouldering embers of the metal bin,

still burning away at the evil weed, the sprinklers above our heads juddering away with water spills. We looked at each other, wet, our shoes soaked with public toilet piss, nervy from all the pressure of this situation, this shit-uation, and burst out laughing, uncontrollably, paroxysms of laughter bolting from our stable doors, laughter reigning magical hilarity all over our faces. We couldn't stop. Nishant did one of his Hammer-time twirls and I jerked forward in an awkward body-popping manoeuvre, and we just laughed.

Nishant looked down into the bin. 'The weed's all burned away,' he said, smiling.

'It's raining in here,' I noted, stifling more giggles.

Nishant held the bin under the tap to wash away any remaining evidence, swilled it out into the sink, the charred remains of illegal drugs, our first and last stash, our first and last illegal activity. He replaced the bin and led me to the door, opening it. It was sunny outside. The trees were whistling, the winds were coursing, children playing.

It was a beautiful day.

*   *   *

We were all wearing the same uniforms. Anand had insisted on wearing his Dr Dre hat. Under the circumstances, Nishant and I decided not to glorify drugs, though couldn't tell Anand why, having made a pact to keep this one little secret from him.

We were wearing our Bleubolts, denim waistcoats – mine had been sent over from India and I'd never taken an interest in it, as it had tassles on the sleeves, which I'd by then cut off – and beige hoodies. Anand was carrying a coconut he'd stolen from his mum's prayer-batch as a visual stimulus. I had my mic technique ready, ready to grip the mic (despite never having used one) between index finger and little finger, resting it on my knuckles. Nishant had slicked up the soles of his feet with Vaseline to make it easier to glide over the stage.

We were ready.

As Auntie Naina said goodbye to my mum and Nishant hovered nearby, I made my way towards the pub. Anand was leaning against the doorframe. He threw up a sideways backwards V sign, which didn't mean 'eff off' in LA; it meant, 'What up SON.' I nodded at him. I was wearing a bandana I'd found from an old cowboy costume from my childhood, luckily blue to match my preferred LA gang affiliation – the Crips, because Snoop Doggy Dogg was down with the Crips. We went inside.

The loud jangle and pow-wow of slot machines cavorted with the spill and tinkle of kegged beers, with the bonhomie of chit-chat, an interesting frequency mix between the unbroken distinctive voices of the teenagers and the gruff old men propping up the bar. It seemed to be divided into two sections. Near the front in the windows were the old men. At the back, towards the conservatory, were the teenagers, hidden from the gaze of the often-passing bobby on the beat. Anand pointed to a sign:

>>>>>>>OPEN MIC THIS WAY

We were directed upstairs, Nishant and Auntie Naina a few footsteps behind. My mind was racing. I wasn't in the zone of actually thinking about performing, though. I caught Pentil's eye as I waded upstairs in a nervy blur. He was sipping on a Guinness and stopped smiling, looking nervous as I passed him.

He should feel nervous, I thought to myself. Thanks to me, all he had to do was lay low and not smoke weed on school premises and find a new connection. The least he could do was stop calling us 'PAKI POSSE' and me 'BLACK BEAUTY'. I could've told Roseblade the whole stinking truth about him, after all.

At the top of the stairs was the sign-up sheet, with ten slots for ten open mic-ers. There was one space left, at the top – ie. the opening act. No one seemed to want to open. I stared at the paper, my competitors, the band names and their descriptions.

1

2 Jamming with Eddy's House Band: bluegrass Public Enemy covers

3 The Harrow Barrow Boys: cheeky cockney songs with a suburban twist

4 Lament of Deathwish: one man heavy metal

5 Johnny Five and the Pizza Bases: jazz-infused baggy indie

6 Melanicole: death maiden torch songs

7 Love Tubs: fat man opera classics

8 Twatfunk Dan: the one man band with a twist – there's two of us!

9 The Fat Controller House Band: local favourites, national treasures

10 Random Amanda: Poet/Death

Nishant stared over my shoulder while Anand fixed his hair under his Dr Dre hat, put on his sunglasses and smiled at a beer mirror. He grabbed the pen . . .

1 Coconut Unlimited: anthems from the street

'What are you doing?' I demanded.

'Well, there's one space left. The best space. Opening. We get up there, show 'em how it's done, go home. They live in our shadow. We get it done. And I think your mum is really mad with you so the quicker the better . . . '

'Yeah but anthems from the street?' It sounded so *whack*.

'Well, it's . . . what shall I put?'

I crossed out 'anthems from the street' and put down 'ghetto hymns'.

'Well, the problem there Mit is we're not Christian. Hymns is like a Christian thing.'

'Yeah, you're right,' I said. 'What then?'

'Ghetto anthems from the street,' Anand said, looking back at us through the mirror.

We bumped fists in agreement.

Eddy emerged holding an old guitar, a beaten leather waistcoast draped round his skinny frame, a tuning fork lodged in his mouth.

'Bloody thing . . . oh hello boys . . . HELLO NAINA!'

'Hi Eddy,' said Nishant's mum, giggling.

'The boys are all in there. Hurry up and grab a glass for the wine on your way to the table.'

Anand and I looked at each other. 'How did Naina know Eddy?' we both wondered silently.

'You boys ready?'

'Yes,' Anand and Nishant chimed in harmony.

'No,' I muttered.

'You're the frontman, Amit. You should be most ready.' Eddy held my shoulder and smiled down at me.

'Yeah man. I know . . . ' I wiped the film of sweat slipping between forehead and bandana.

'Listen, before we go in, you've remembered what your *birthdays* are?'

'We're all sixteen,' Nishant smiled, looking impossibly young.

'Good lads. Have a cracker!' He glanced at the sheet. 'First, eh? Cracking.' He smiled encouragingly and went back into the room.

I held out my fists for a prolonged bump. We dapped our knuckles together, ready.

'Listen, boys. This is Coconut Unlimited. There is no escaping. We are billeted, styles filleted. Ya get me? We are rocking this joint, we are running this town. Seen?'

'SEEN!' they back-sang at me.

Nishant practised a twirl. Anand threw up another gang sign. 'Ready.'

We strode in.

*   *   *

It was mostly old men inside, all standing about in denim and leather waistcoats. They turned to look at us. Silence.

'We all sixteen!' Anand shouted.

The room nodded collectively and carried on their conversations. I stared at the stage, then at the crowd. We were the youngest in the room. The next oldest was . . . probably Melanicole, who could've been any age really, under all that goth make-up she was wearing. The rest of them looked like weirdo townies and old clapped-out rockers. This was weird.

Maybe one of the clapped out rockers was a talent scout for Death Row Records or something. Play every gig like it's the most important one. That was the advice Eddy had given me.

We didn't know where to stand so stood in the centre of the crowd space. Nishant waved to his mum, drinking with Eddy and his band. The whole room was full of Eddy-types. It couldn't be right. Was this where our fortunes were going to be made?

'Buzzing crowd tonight!' Nishant grinned.

'That's their artifical hearts, man,' Anand snorted. 'They geriatric and shit.'

'Play every gig like it's the most important one,' I said sagely, rooted to the spot, not really sure what to do with myself.

'Listen Mit,' Anand grinned. 'I'm just roadtesting at this stage. Try everything on these fools here and see what sticks before jamming my takings elsewhere. That's what Meena says.'

She was trying to take the band away from me, I knew it. She wanted her guy to be the frontman. I wondered why she didn't want *me* – the actual frontman.

'After this gig,' Anand said, 'I might work on my solo album for a bit you know. Do my own thing . . . '

'We've not even done our own album,' I said, shaking my head.

A fat man wearing a T-shirt with the Fat Controller steam-pressed on it approached the microphone, holding a pint of stout. The crowd hushed.

'Alright,' he said in a tiny voice. He had army trousers on and grey socks, no shoes – ie. no swagger. He was red and pale simultaneously, his greying thick hair matching his socks, nails bruised and calloused fingertips gripping the beer glass. 'It's

Monday, it's open, it's mic. It's yours and mine.' He was going through the motions, a veteran of the Harrow music scene. 'A few new faces tonight – I've been assured by their mum they're all over sixteen . . . all from the same family too I bet. Some familiar faces as well. Alright Jonjo . . . ' He motioned somewhere out into the audience. 'I thought I barred you for doing a Cure cover? You know I hate the Cure! Anyway, without further ado, can we give a warm Fat Controller first-timer welcome to anthemic ghetto hymnal street rappers . . . Coconut Unlimited!'

There was a smattering of applause, and we were on. Quick-focus. It'd all happened too quickly, and I hadn't collected myself. Nishant rushed forwards with the tape we needed playing, Anand grabbed a second microphone and practised gripping it while I stood in the middle of the floor, staring at the stage. I pushed myself on. I willed myself on. Nishant and the Fat Controller guy scrabbled around lifting up a tape recorder from behind the bar and moving it to the stage, connecting it up. Anand was pulling me towards him, still gripping the microphone, feedback from him covering it, from being in front of the speakers, a grimace on his face that spoke of years of hardship in the ghetto. I relented. A murmur echoed around the room in the near silence of sorting out our technical requirements. I stood behind the microphone, running through the lyrics in my head, worrying about the half-remembered bits, trying desperately to remember the flow, how to ride the beat, how to do this thing. What the hell was happening? My mouth was dry, my lips coarse, my tongue thick, and I couldn't remember a single thing. My mind was empty, my muscles buzzing, my feet overheating. I couldn't remember a single thing.

'Ready?'

I looked up. Nishant was taking position behind me. The Fat Controller guy was hovering his fingers over the 'play' button. Eff it, I thought, and grabbed the microphone. I looked around me. People were still talking as I heard the crackle of the blank start of the tape. Anand commanded the crowd pay attention.

'LISTEN!' he boomed. 'It's Coconut Unlimited, get me?'

People turned their heads to acknowledge the stage. The tape recorder started pumping out the Nas beat for 'It Ain't Hard to Tell' semi-quietely, and I begin by announcing us.

> *It's Coconut Unlimited*
> *I'm Mit Dogg. I'm Coconut Unlimited*
> *MC AP is Coconut Unlimited*

[That's ME!]

> *DJ Dangerous is Coconut Unlimited*

I couldn't see what Nishant was doing but I could feel him moving about wildly behind me. People maintained only half-attention. I launched into my lyrics. Hard. I stared at my trainers, occasionally looking up to gauge reactions, faltering slightly as I did. My heart was pounding, the quiet tape recorder humming at full volume and the sound of the squeaks of Nishant's trainers on the floor distracting me.

By the time the first chorus came, we'd lost the crowd. You could just tell. Anand was pushing all over the stage wildly, cavorting his body in every direction, pointing his crotch to Meena, standing by the door, nodding. I was completely still, just looking at the ground. Nishant was doing something behind me, I didn't know what.

And this was Coconut Unlimited. It was badness personified. And not in a good way – the hip-hop way. What the hell? Why didn't these people care? The hum of their chatter was louder than my backing track and I kept falling out of time with the beat, and couldn't keep the lyrics up. That was it. I was vexed.

'You lot have NO RESPECT!' I shouted, losing patience. People just talked louder. 'Dangerous stop the tape!'

Nishant stumbled in a spin and turned the tape recorder off. There was a hum, chatter, a smattering of applause, assuming we'd finished.

'You peoples have no respect for the artist. No respect for me or my crew. We come here, we bring the badness to you, and

187

you're just sat talking about your accounts or some shit with your peoples. You know what? You want skills? I got skills and bars . . . FREESTYLE . . .

> *No respect, bruv you got no respect*
> *I detect you elect a speck deck*
> *Wreck your crew, I can't respect you*
> *You got no respect . . .*
> *You got NO RESPECT*
> *NORESPECTNORESPECTNORESPECTNO*
> *RESPECTNORESPECT*

I looked to Anand to back me up, drop in some adlibs and backing vocals for my freestyle, but he was replacing his microphone on the stand and shaking his head at my screaming.

I was mad, I was livid, I was shouting at the top of my voice. Everyone was definitely looking at me now. Shouting stuff I couldn't hear. Replying to my screams.

No respect. They had no respect for me. I'd come here, I'd sweated blood to be here, I'd nearly compromised everything to be here, given it my all and still they were apathetic. I was convinced. It was cos they were racist.

'Listen, people of Harrow,' I said, calming down a bit. 'I know you ain't know what it's like to live on the street . . . so HAVE SOME RESPECT!'

Silence.

'Don't you go to private school with my son?' someone shouted.

Cue laughter.

I dropped the microphone on the door and ran towards the door, shoving into Meena on my way. Nishant followed me, while Anand shook his head and bounded over to Meena to kiss her. She held his face, telling him how well he did, and he shook his head as I rushed back down the stairs. I could hear the murmur of the compere retrieving the microphone.

'Amit . . . AMIT!' Nishant called after me. 'It's all good. It's raw. First time. You were nervous . . . '

'Nah, mate, we were *whack*. You get me?' I said, not even trying the rudebwoy accent, just normally, half-heartedly, like it didn't matter anymore. Which it didn't. I bumped into a wet sensation at the bottom of the stairs, a bump and a slosh and wetness down my hoodie. I turned round. It was Pentil.

'What the fuck Chuckles?'

'Up yours Pentil. You milk bottle, get out of my way.'

'Piss off shrimp. Get outta here. You're not welcome, go back to where you came from.'

'Racist!' I screamed.

'If I'm racist, who's my Asian friend?'

'Who? That coconut over there?' I pointed at Jasel. 'He's just your excuse you prick.'

'I'm not a racist. I just hate seafood. Shrimps like you. Shrimp curry face.'

'Whatever, just be glad I didn't get you expelled . . . '

'What? What the fuck did you just say?'

'I said up yours!' I pushed past him and did this sideways punch, like I was banging a resistant lego brick into formation in Pentil's side. He keeled to his right and squealed. The pub looked over at me and him and all the old men started heckling us.

I ran towards the door and Jasel grabbed my arm and pulled me back in, then I raised my still-clenched fist in the middle of all the mêlée. He held up a 'one minute' finger and ran towards Pentil, kneed him in the side till he fell over then kicked him. The old men left their stools to sort us out, as Nishant was pleading with me to get out of there. I looked at an old man running towards me with a stool screaming 'NOT AGAIN NOT AGAIN' and Jasel ran back towards me, pushed me out the door and we all ran to my mum's car.

Nishant paused at the door. 'Mum!' He ran back in. I ran to follow, to get Nishant. Jasel stopped me.

'Let me go, man, that's my boy . . . '

'He'll be fine. Look Amit, we cool yeah? No hard feelings?'

'What for? Making my life a living hell?'

'Man, that was just jokes . . . '

'Is this still an apology?'

'Look, I get it. We need to stick together. Brothers and ting.'

'I ain't your brother, understood?'

'You know what I mean. Listen man, lighten up . . . '

'Lighten up? I go to a school where everyone takes the piss out of me for either being quiet or being poor or being a Paki, but mostly for being a Paki. Then you join and I think cool, safety in numbers. But you turn out to be a prick. Then I decide I like something different from everyone else and you spend the whole thing rinsing me for it. Brothers? Whatever bruv.'

'Well we stick together now, yeah?'

'Whatever dude. You go your own path.'

I pushed him away and opened the passenger seat of Mum's car, spotting Nishant bursting out of the pub with his mum and Anand behind clamping onto Meena. They took off towards St George's, while Nishant and his mum pounded into our car.

Mum drove away, with no sense of urgency, as the old men of the pub erupted into the street, screaming.

Nishant tapped me on the shoulder affectionately. 'Hey Amit, you were right. They had no respect.'

Next: Back in the day when I
was young . . . I'm not a kid anymore

EPILOGUE

Awards Tour

The car bounces along, erratic, a million miles away from my slow start.

Anand's driving is louder than the stereo volume that thumps and clutters as he bounces his head. I reach over him and turn the volume down.

'Hey Nandy,' I say. 'You got any Coconut Unlimited?'

'Nah man, but those guys were *pretty cool*,' he says, nodding. 'You know they only ever did one mixtape together? Legendary status . . . ' He smiles and turns the volume back up.

The journey's syncopated by what Anand calls his 'reminix-tapes' – songs from our teendom, mostly the same tapes we used to make for each other in the days of the band, now transferred to CD. He grins at us when each new song becomes recognisable.

Nishant snoozes, still tired from flying, and I stare out of the window at the gloomily-familiar North Circular Road as the inevitable Harrow approaches. Hello old friend. The industrial warehouses, the superstores and the noodles of traffic all pass by as I rest my hot face on the cool window pane.

Harrow town centre looms. We pass Saqee, the Indian restaurant owned by Anand's uncle. It was where we had our final meal as a three, before Nishant moved to Paris, his dad having landed a job at Disneyland. He moved to Atlanta three years later, then to Portland and then, after seven years in America, Thailand, where he now works as a homeopathic doctor. He seems settled now, just about, but the itchiness in his feet has never gone away.

A memory flashes through my head: the three of us standing

outside, as Anand's uncle snaps the photograph I now have in my house. We all clowned for the camera, then Nishant left to discover the world. Anand and I carried on as before, more co-dependent in Nishant's absence.

My phone keeps beeping confirmations for tonight's activities, littered with stag-threats – 'we're gonna get you drunk and do a variety of humiliating things to you', etc. I ignore them and write Alice a message, telling her that we're on our way to our first destination, and that I love her.

*   *   *

Months earlier Anand had called me, upset. He'd come over to meet me at my local. I wasn't gigging that night so met with him and he told me, in tears, that he felt he'd wasted his life. He'd settled into a job in local business marketing, earning the bare minimum to afford a singleton's life: a car, and a cheap flat within walking distance of his mum and dad's, thereby drastically reducing his food bill. He wanted to know what had happened, why life had passed him by and why I was getting married and he was the single one.

'We should swap lives man,' he grinned.

'You can't have Alice,' I said, smiling.

'No man, I be the rock star shagging all the girls interested in my attentions and you have my local job and local life and be married and happy.'

'I'm a performance poet, bruv. What makes you think I get girls interested in my attentions? I'm no Arctic Monkey. I'm not even Keane.'

'You just referenced two bands I got no idea about, blud. All I'm saying is: I'll gig every night and chase tail. You be married with a desk job . . . '

'You know it doesn't work like that,' I said, interrupting.

'We were going to rule the world . . . '

'Imagine that . . . ' I replied, quoting Nas.

He slept over that night, too drunk to work the sofa bed. In the morning, I called in sick for him, giving the familiar 'diarrhoea' excuse we'd worked into a fine art. When it was time to part, for him to go home and me to a library in Brixton for my poetry group, he gave me a cuddle, something he only did on special occasions.

I watched him get into his car from my front window vantage point, and couldn't help but feel sad.

*   *   *

Back in the car, reliving our shared experiences through music and same-same anecdotes feels more comfortable than I imagined it would. I usually groan whenever Alice and her university friends leap into their usual 'remember when' conversations, something I'm excluded from, having not gone to university with them. Now I wonder if shared experiences are all we have after a while; shared experiences and cultural reference points.

I'm about to get married. Things are about to change and yet I'm reliving my 14-year-old life, allowing someone else's shared experience of gangsta rap fuel my shared experiences with Anand and Nishant. Is it bizarre that this of all things can take us back? Something we only ever appreciated, never really understood.

Maudlin minute over, I ask Nishant how his new girlfriend is.

Having recently reconnected through the power of Skype, social networking and email chat relays, we'd caught up a little. I hadn't seen him since, as a fifteen-year-old, I'd visited the village near Disneyland he'd moved to. I'd since learned about his drink-driving incident, his absconding from college to Portland to make candles with a hippie girl he loved then married then divorced, then his becoming a doctor of homeopathic medicine and, six months ago, his moving to Thailand.

He'd rescued his now-girlfriend from a potentially loveless marriage by crashing it, film-style, shouting 'I DO' when the inevitable and awkward 'does anyone know of any reason why these two should not be joined in matrimony?' question was asked, running down the aisle, telling her that she needed to be with him instead of the douchebag she was about to marry, and subsequently having a torrid affair. Somehow, Nishant had lived adventures enough for all three of us.

I'd gone down the path we'd all planned, but only as a form of rebellion. It was clichéd how it all came about. I did a law degree, thanks to my dad's objectives>targets>goal life formula. I needed a proper job, he'd decided, and people would always need doctors, lawyers and teachers. Doctoring required a knowledge of science and maths and teaching wasn't very well paid, so lawyering it was. I acquiesced, having a crying breakdown on my second day and telling everyone I wanted to do English, them telling me that if I wanted to do English I could, and me shouting that they didn't understand the dynamics of my family structure.

Life moved in strange concentric circles for three years as I resigned myself to my fate. I did law half-heartedly, had a few half-hearted relationships with half-hearted girls, lusted after Hilary, an Irish redhead, lusted after Elena who did law too, till I had a conversation with her on a train and decided she was boring, because the only thing we had in common was law.

I went to the same barber every month because of a beautiful Australian girl. I never managed to time getting my hair cut by her, ending up getting looked after by a bald German with tattoos on his head, who did a stoic and fantastic job of teasing out my fringe. The only time I got her, she gave me a fashionable mullet without asking and I had her shave it all off, which led to a depressing period of my life with an internet girlfriend as my only solace.

Rapping had disappeared from my worldview. The internet girlfriend became my excuse for never going out, or for leaving early because I had to be at home at 10 p.m. every night to talk to her online. I still lived with my mum and dad at the time, unhappy about the direction of my life. Mum would tell me that happiness was secondary to stability.

Eventually, Dad would ask me what I could do that would make me happy. He urged me to go into journalism after university.

Then I had another epiphany. I went to see a *pretty cool* Asian drum'n'bass punk band of seasoned musicians, and a chance meeting with the lead singer after the concert reignited my love of rap.

I suddenly wanted to perform. I wanted to get onstage and wipe away the 'NO RESPECT' incident, which had passed into modern folklore among friends due to Anand repeatedly bringing it up as an icebreaker.

I left university, worked at Gap while I decided what to do with my life, telling Mum and Dad I wanted a year off my law degree, having scraped a 2.2. I worked there, I rapped, I met a DJ called Rob and his brother Tom and we did gigs together. We were OK. I was fuelled by the energy of knowing that if a *pretty cool* all-Asian drum'n'bass punk band could be semi-famous, then so could I.

I eventually fell into poetry gigs, learning, finally, that I lacked the necessary swagger to be a rapper. The poet's life was exactly what I was looking for and, five years after leaving university a depressed and broken man, I was working from my kitchen, gigging regularly and engaged to a curly-haired white teacher.

I was comfortable. Mum was happy, Dad was happy that I was happy, and I understood them both.

Dad's business, which had been his obsession, had folded and he was working in semi-retirement at a book charity. He finally understood what I was on about when I insisted on doing things that made me smile, and I finally appreciated the sacrifices he'd made to send me to a private school and give me that choice. I was apologetic about not making a return on his investment. We met for drinks and had a social life together. We were in sync now. I even wrote a book of poetry about him called *Stories My Dad Tells* – fantastical alternative realities of his life based on his stock phrases and sentiments.

Sitting here now, on our way to the mystery location, I think about our teenage years and the delusions we lived under, and laugh. I used to be embarrassed by remembrances of myself but now I'm at ease.

It's funny to think that, in a way, I've managed to stick to my guns, my plans.

I think about my diametrically opposed realities: the lawyer and the rapper; the desk job and the stage job. I wonder which decisions in my life led me away from these possibilities.

I think about Anand and Nishant and where they've been in the last fifteen years. I'm the middle one, I realise now. The one who got away but returns enough to remember. I couldn't be on Nishant's trajectory, but I couldn't be in Anand's static. I'm content.

I close my eyes. This day is already perfect. The bam of the boom-bap on Anand's far-from-tinny stereo and seeing the familiar just-woke-up fuzz of Nishant's hair, Anand's tiny monkey ears, the Ganesha idol sticky-padded to his dashboard – a request of his mum to keep him safe. He'd never admit it but he's become more religious, more cultured, as he's got older. It's something to do with wanting to find someone, I think. He's asked his mum to assist him with Gujarati introductions, something I never thought he'd do. When he told me, he expressed surprise at how clear he was about the decision. I'm happy for him. He's finding himself at last, and he's been lost the longest.

Nishant gazes back at me and catches me in a pensive moment. I reach out my hand for the handslap greeting we developed, which always ends in a thumb war.

He remembers it.

*   *   *

We're stuck in traffic. Anand turns to us both, in our contemplative silences, lowers the volume on the stereo and speaks slowly. 'Listen, boys. Now we're all here, I've got a confession . . . '

'You're gay?' I say.

'I'm engaged.'

Nishant and I just look at each other, and I mime a dropped jaw for effect.

'Congratulations?' Nishant offers.

'Wait. I'm engaged. . . to Meena.'

'What the what?'

I can't believe it. They've had a fraught fifteen years of him loathing her, shagging her, being dumped by her in a variety of humiliating situations involving camel rides, a bouncy castle, a milkshake for two at a country cottage and, most recently, my parents' anniversary party. This is probably not a healthy thing for a man struggling to shake off the shackles of the past and move on with his life. Especially with someone as repulsive as Meena.

I want to say something but Anand's looking for support. I tap his hand and he smiles.

'I know Mit Dogg thinks I'm a fucking idiot. . . '

'She's got no respect for you man . . . '

'NO RESPECT NO RESPECT NO RESPECT!' Nishant bursts in, and we all laugh at that crystallised remembered moment of our teen years.

'Listen, Nishant. Let me tell you a story about adult Meena. She hexed Anand. Yes, that's right, hexed him. Her aunt's into black magic. One night while Anand's sleeping, she shaves his eyebrows, for the hair, and puts a spell on him that he'll be true to her. She makes a bowl of pilau, adding this concoction of his hair and other bits to it. Then, while it's hot, she squats over it so the sweat from her . . . *bits*, falls into the pilau rice. This sweat rice concoction is meant to tie his body to hers forever. She's a headcase. This was only last week. Now they're engaged!'

Nishant is stifling laughter, not sure whether I've just told him a lie or not. He places a tender hand on Anand's shoulder, a move that breaks my heart. No matter what the situation is, Nishant will always make sure you're OK. 'Sorry to hear that Anand,' he says, sweetly.

197

'It's OK, really Nishant. To be honest . . . the sex is amazing.'

'Is that before or after you've eaten her sweat rice?' Nishant says, exploding in giggles.

'So you're really getting married?' I ask, still shocked.

'Yeah man. It was about time. Mum reckons she's just wild cos no one's tamed her. I should put a ring on her finger . . . '

'Is your mum borrowing advice from Beyoncé now?' Nishant interrupts.

We laugh again, the bonhomie thick in the air. I'm not sure Anand should marry such a weirdo but then he's grinning from small ear to small ear, and in the last fifteen years it's the happiest I've seen him.

'Anand,' I whisper, after a while. 'She still can't come to the wedding . . . '

'But she's practically family, man!'

*   *   *

We stop in a Harrow car park, behind the shopping centre, and roll through the centre of town. I know where we're headed but let Anand misdirect us. He points to various failings of classmates.

'Pentil's the manager of that Costa. He always gives me 10% off . . . '

'He has to,' I interrupt. 'Your office is above it.'

We wade through the town. I'm silent, but Anand's happily chatting away, updating Nishant on people he half-remembers from our school days. He updates him on Ahmed, who now works in a care home, and how his little brother grew up to be a rapper; he tells him about Herman, about how we never heard from Jasel again; about teachers been and gone; about Meena; about Ravi embezzling funds from the Young Gujaratis of North London Society. Nishant nods – I can't decide if he's feigning interest or not, whether he remembers these guys.

'The Fat Controller!' Anand says, erupting with the reveal of his long-kept secret. Nishant slaps his back.

'What a surprise, Nandy,' I say, mock-disappointed.

He furrows his brow. 'You knew?'

'Of course man.'

'OK well let's cancel and do something else. Plan B . . . '

'No man,' I interrupt. 'It's all good. The Fat Controller. I love it.'

'Good . . . cos there is no Plan B!'

He leads us through into the pub. The clientele has changed a lot since our first gig here. It's all old Indian men and Kingfisher on tap. Migrant gentrification. I haven't been here in years. The décor is the same, but faded, celebrations of premium lagers and sports (though the preference is now cricket rather than football). The bar and walls are coloured in a vomit-inducing orange and lilac combo and the tables still sticky with the grease of fat controllers, now just ghosts. We walk through towards the upstairs venue. I smile at Anand as he pounds up the stairs, stopping and offering a cheeky grin.

Then I read the sign on the door. Anand raps it loudly, three times. It says: 'FOR ONE NIGHT ONLY – COCONUT UNLIMITED REUNION.'

I smile. Oh no . . . oh dear . . . oh wow . . .

Anand bursts through, Nishant does a Michael Jackson spin and I follow to a massive cheer and people screaming 'NO RESPECT NO RESPECT NO RESPECT'. I see Rob behind some decks. He scratches a DUF–DUF–D–D–D–DUFF and the instrumental for 'It Ain't Hard to Tell' by Nas comes on, pounding through the speakers. Everyone cheers.

All my friends and family, my dad, Alice's dad, are all huddled at a table. I look at my best friends going wild around me, at the Coconut Unlimited banner done in Nishant's original design and at Rob, dressed as a Crip, winking at me, and all this nostalgia, all this memory – it's what makes a man.

The drums are pounding, everyone's waving their hands from side to side, the bassline's funking Anand's feet in all directions as he declares our bandname loudly. Nishant is lost in a trance of his own moves. The drums, the bass, the samples, the rhythm and the riddims – all it needs is some bars, some lyrics, some spits, some bam.

I'm handed a microphone and, for a pregnant pause, I imagine the reunion concert is going on in my head. I pull the mic to my lips, gripped between index and little finger, resting on my knuckles.

Dangerous drops the beat, I drop heat
Like a pile of burning spaghetti on your white sheets . . .